Get ready to
by perfect

Mills & Boon
fabulous, heart-warming reads
by bestselling author

Jessica Steele

Jessica's classic love stories will whisk you
into a world of pure romantic excitement…

Recent titles by this author:

A MOST SUITABLE WIFE
VACANCY: A WIFE OF CONVENIENCE

PROMISE OF
A FAMILY

BY
JESSICA STEELE

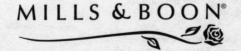

MILLS & BOON®

All the characters in this book have no existence outside the imagination of the author, and have no relation whatsoever to anyone bearing the same name or names. They are not even distantly inspired by any individual known or unknown to the author, and all the incidents are pure invention.

First published in Great Britain 2006
Harlequin Mills & Boon Limited,
Eton House, 18-24 Paradise Road, Richmond, Surrey TW9 1SR

© Jessica Steele 2006

Standard ISBN: 0 263 84926 0
Promotional ISBN: 0 263 85482 5

Set in Times Roman 10½ on 12pt
02-1006-56105

Printed and bound in Spain
by Litografia Rosés, S.A., Barcelona

Jessica Steele lives in the county of Worcestershire, with her super husband, Peter, and their gorgeous Staffordshire bull terrier, Florence. Any spare time is spent enjoying her three main hobbies: reading espionage novels, gardening (she has a great love of flowers), and playing golf. Any time left over is celebrated with her fourth hobby, shopping. Jessica has a sister and two brothers, and they all, with their spouses, often go on golfing holidays together. Having travelled to various places on the globe, researching background for her stories, there are many countries that she would like to revisit. Her most recent trip abroad was to Portugal, where she stayed in a lovely hotel, close to her all-time favourite golf course. Jessica had no idea of being a writer until one day Peter suggested she write a book. So she did. She has now written over eighty novels.

... ...

CHAPTER ONE

THEY were in the kitchen of the large, rambling old house when, sensing her niece's eyes on her—her half-niece, to be exact—Leyne looked up from the school uniform shirt she was ironing.

'What?' she asked, looking into Pip's direct gaze.

Pip stared at her for a few more seconds and then, reddening slightly, said in a rush, 'Leyne—do you know who my father is?'

The question was so totally unexpected that Leyne felt winded by it and was not sure that her jaw did not drop a fraction. Pip had never shown any curiosity about her father before, and now of all times, with her mother out of the country, was not the best time for her to start asking questions on that subject.

'Er—no, love, I don't,' Leyne replied honestly.

'Mmm.' Pip accepted her answer and went on to ask a question in connection with the history project she was working on and needed for school in the morning.

Leyne hoped that the question of who Pip's father was had been an idle, throw-away kind of question. But as she lay in her bed that night she could not get out of her mind that direct look of her half-sister's eleven-and-a-half-year-old daughter.

In the normal way of things, and Leyne admitted she was biased, Pip was the most loveable and amenable child. But occasionally, only very occasionally, she would get that direct look in her gorgeous green eyes. Direct as well as stubborn, if she did not know the answer to why, or who, or whatever, she would chip away until she did have the answer she wanted.

Still hoping that her niece's question the previous evening had been an idle one, Leyne dropped her and her friend Alice off at their school the next morning. From there she drove to her job as assistant management accountant, with her head in a jumble of thoughts.

Maxine, Pip's mother, had gone off on an extended working trip less than a week ago. 'Are you sure you'll be able to cope?' Max had only yesterday insisted when she had phoned from the airport in Madrid.

Max had at first decided against taking up the fantastic chance to accompany Ben Turnbull, one of the world's leading photographers, when, recovering from a motor accident, he'd had to face the unpalatable fact that he would either have to take an assistant or cancel the six-month-long trip. But apparently there was no way he was prepared to cancel all his preparations, even if he had to take two assistants.

Max, given the set-backs that went with being a single parent, was, at thirty-five, something of a photographer in her own right, and her name must have reached the great Ben Turnbull's ears. Because it was quite out of the blue that a letter had arrived addressed to Max Nicholson. And, her work speaking for itself, it seemed, Ben Turnbull, either still recovering or not condescending to interview her, had, without an interview, astonishingly offered her the job any photographer worthy of the name would give their eye-teeth for.

Leyne remembered the way Max's eyes had lit up, recalled her yelp of joy when she'd read of the offer: six months, possibly longer, worldwide trip, expenses paid, salary paid, with the chance thrown in to photograph animals in their native surrounds, landscapes, wild flowers, indigenous tribespeople—Max had been near to drooling as she had read on.

It had not taken her long, however, to realise that there was no way that she could accept the awesome job offer. 'No,' she had decided as reality forced its ugly way in through what she had soon seen was just one huge, big fantastic dream. 'It's not on.'

'Why isn't it?' Leyne had asked, feeling her half-sister's disappointment as though it were her own.

'You need to ask?' Max had replied, her eyes going to the beautiful black-and-white portrait of her daughter Philippa she had taken only a few months ago.

'You—um—wouldn't trust Pip with me?' Leyne had asked.

'Trust you! Of course I would, silly! Why, you probably have more to do with her than I do! Especially when I'm off on one of my assignments.'

'I've looked after Pip when you've been away before,' Leyne agreed. 'And you know it's no problem for me to work from home if need be. In fact, with the move to larger premises still on hold, they'll be glad of extra desk space if I need to be home for any reason. Couldn't this be just another of your assignments?'

Max stared at her, and Leyne just knew that her sister was beginning to rethink. 'But I've never had an assignment that lasted as long as six months before,' she pointed out—weakening fast; this once-in-a-lifetime opportunity was unlikely to ever come her way again.

'Neither can you ignore this wonderful chance,' Leyne urged, not forgetting the thrilled light of excitement that had shone in Max's eyes when she had first read her letter. 'And, aside from this splendid chance, your name would be even more well known when you get back.'

'If only I could take Pip with me,' Max fretted.

'I'd hate it if you did,' Leyne said quietly.

'You're a second mum to her.' Max smiled.

'Who could help but love her?' Leyne commented simply, and was silent for a few moments as she recalled how, shortly after her father had died, Pip had been born. She had been the most adorable baby, and for Leyne it had been love at first sight. Having just lost her father, and being the same eleven and a half years old that Pip now was, Leyne had loved, worried and fretted over the baby's smallest tummy ache from day one. If Miss Philippa Nicholson had been sent to help Leyne over the death of her much-loved father, her arrival could not have been more timely.

'Pip has settled well into her new school.' Max talked through the plus points. Her daughter, eleven last April, had moved to senior school a month ago, at the start of the September term. 'And she seems to be growing out of her asthma. But—oh, I don't know, Leyne. It seems an awful nerve to leave her with you while I go globetrotting, not to say the wrench it will be to leave her, to leave you both.'

Looking at her dear half-sister, Leyne could see that Max was being torn in two with indecision. Life had not been easy for her, could not have been, bringing up Pip on her own. For all Leyne, and their mother, initially, had been there to help, the burden of responsibility for the jewel in all their lives ultimately still belonged with Max.

'Look at it from the other angle,' Leyne suggested. 'What will it mean to your career if you *do* go?'

Max considered the question, and then answered, 'Well, aside from the invaluable experience I should gain working with Ben Turnbull, and the professional feather in my cap it would be to be able to say I worked with him for months on end, I'd be able to do my own stuff if I went, photograph in places I've only ever imagined, and...' Her eyes went dreamy again before, making a determined effort, Max brought herself back to the practicalities. 'And I should start reaping some financial rewards. Pip, even at her tender age, has started taking an interest in clothes, and I should like the chance to indulge her rather than have to tell her she can't have something because we simply can't afford it.'

Over coffee they talked about it, around it, and of it, and it was oh, so clear to Leyne that her sister must go, that she must not turn down this superb opportunity. But in the end it was Leyne who suggested, 'While not putting the onus on Pip, why not casually mention it to her and see how she would feel about you going?'

'I'd hate you to go,' was Pip's reaction. But, like the darling she was, 'But I'd hate it much, much more if you didn't go because of me.'

'I've always said you're the best daughter a mother ever had,' Max responded fondly.

Pip grinned. 'I'd come with you if I could, but someone has to stay home and look out for Leyne.'

The decision, it seemed, was made. Yet, still the same, the last time the two half-sisters were alone together Max repeated her question of, 'Are you sure you're all right about me going and leaving Pip with you?'

'Stop worrying. She'll be fine. We'll both be fine.'

'What if she starts going through that stroppy stage?'

'Stroppy? Pip? You're looking for problems.'

'I'm not, honestly. I was talking to Dianne Gardner only the other day, and she was telling me that Alice has started to be something of a little madam since she and Pip started at their new school.'

'I can't see it, but if it happens I'll deal with it,' Leyne had promised. And, in an attempt to reassure, 'And anything else that might or might not crop up.'

But now, as she parked her car at Paget and Company, Leyne could not help wondering if she *could* deal with anything that cropped up. Crossing her fingers that Pip's 'Do you know who my father is?' question had been nothing more than a passing notion of a question, Leyne went into her office. Pip's friend's parents were divorced, and Alice had spent last weekend with her father—perhaps the two girls had been discussing fathers that day. Or perhaps they were having more adult lessons now they had moved to the senior school, and something in class had triggered the question.

Leyne's morning was interrupted when Keith Collins, one of the accountants newly arrived at Paget and Company a few months previously, and a man she had started dating some weeks ago, came in to see her.

'Fancy joining me for a sumptuous dinner this evening?' he enquired.

His invitation was a touch unfair, Leyne considered. He must know that too—they had barely started going out when she'd had to put a few spokes in the smooth running of the dating wheel. She and Dianne Gardner, Alice's mother, had a mutually satisfactory arrangement when it came to having a social life and organising child welfare. To go out that evening would mean leaving Pip with Dianne. But Leyne did not care for Pip's bedtime routine to be interrupted when there was school the next day.

'The idea is lovely, the practicalities a touch unmanageable,' she declined as nicely as she could. 'You could come and have supper with Pip and me, though, if you like.'

Keith did not like.

'His loss.' Pip grinned over a salmon *en croûte* supper that night, when Leyne mentioned she had invited Keith Collins to share their meal but how he 'hadn't been free'.

Leyne went to bed in a happier frame of mind.

Max, with the portrait of her daughter packed in her luggage, had taken off from Madrid en route to Brazil, and must have landed in Rio by now. And Pip had not pursued her question of who her father was.

Max phoned the next night. Everything was well, she said, adding that she and Ben Turnbull were tolerating each other.

'Tolerating?' Leyne queried, and only then learned that Ben Turnbull had apparently been expecting a male Max Nicholson, and had been staggered to find himself stuck with a very feminine Maxine Nicholson, and with no time to find a replacement who'd had all the necessary vaccinations for foreign parts. Realising that he would have dumped her had he been able, had caused Max to metaphorically dig her heels in. While she might not like the wretched man, and given the tons of photography equipment she had to carry, she was determined to show him that she could do the job required of her every bit as well as some male counterpart. Her excitement at the prospect of the work and adventure before her was undiminished. Leyne handed the phone over to Pip so she should chat with her mother, with every confidence that Max, with the bit between her teeth, so to speak, would do exactly that.

Leyne was not feeling so happy the following evening, though. Dianne Gardner had collected Pip from school with her daughter Alice. Leyne collected

Pip on her way home from her office, and, 'Leyne?' Pip began seriously the moment they were indoors.

'Pip?' Leyne enquired, her mind more on what they were going to have for supper than what was on her niece's mind.

'Do you know why my father has never been to see me?'

Oh, sweetheart, Leyne mourned, even as her spirits plummeted. 'I don't, Pip, I'm sorry,' she apologised. 'Perhaps he and your mother had a bad falling-out.'

Her niece was silent for a while as she considered Leyne's reply, but was soon giving Leyne more cause for disquiet when she went on to solemnly ask, 'Leyne, if you truly don't know who my father is, do you think you could find out?'

Oh, heavens—how did she handle this? Leyne looked at her, looked into those lovely green eyes. 'It's—um—important, is it, chick?' she returned lightly. 'I mean, do you think you could wait until your mum comes home?'

Pip did not need to think about it for very long. 'No. I don't think I could,' she answered gravely. 'I've wanted to know who he is for some while, but—well, Mum was always so busy, and I rather think I was a bit embarrassed too to ask. And, well, I don't think I could wait endless months until Mum gets back.'

Leyne studied her niece's earnest little face, and

just had to go to her and give her a hug. 'It might take me some little while,' she hedged. 'But can you leave it with me, and I'll see what I can do?'

'I knew you would,' Pip responded trustingly—and Leyne felt her heart would break. How long had this been fidgeting away in the dear child's head?

Leyne wondered what could she do? Goodness knew when Max would be in touch again. Should she try to contact her on her cellphone? Why not? Max, after all, was the only person to tell her, and also to tell her how she wanted her to handle this delicate situation.

Leyne waited until Pip had been in bed an hour before, calculating that it would be around seven in the evening in Brazil, she rang her sister's mobile phone number.

Her hope, however, that she would not be ringing Max in the middle of something extremely important was not required. Her sister's phone was on voicemail, and Leyne realised Max must have switched it off.

Over the next few days, very much aware of how frequently Pip would give her that serious-eyed look, Leyne tried to contact her sister. But each time she met with the same result. Max's phone was never switched on.

With Pip's silently questioning eyes starting to haunt her, Leyne gave serious thought to calling the emergency contact number Max had left. But would Max or, by the sound of it, grumpy Ben Turnbull appreciate some runner chasing after them in some dense jungle—or wherever they might be—with the domestic question of who was Max's child's father?

It was a dilemma that caused Leyne to have some very fitful nights. But, whatever she did, she knew that she must not panic. She must deal with this as she had so glibly told Max that she could deal with anything that cropped up. She must deal with it calmly and without fuss. But where the Dickens did she start if she was to try not to send someone racing after Max when she had barely just left on her six-month-long assignment?

'I suppose you're busy tomorrow?' Keith Collins asked when he stopped by Leyne's desk on Friday.

Pip was having a sleepover at Alice Gardner's home tomorrow. 'Depends why?' Leyne replied with a smile.

'I was thinking dinner—and then coffee at my place?'

Leyne wasn't so very sure about the coffee offer. While she did not doubt that Keith was quite capable of making them coffee, it was what went with the coffee that she was wary of. She liked Keith, but was only starting to get to know him.

'Dinner sounds lovely,' she accepted.

'I'll call for you at seven,' he replied, with a wolfish kind of grin, and went on his way.

Leyne supposed she was still half hoping that Pip was not truly serious about wanting to know the identity of her father. But, on picking her up from Dianne Gardner's house after work, Leyne soon realised that her niece was far from ready to let go.

'I don't suppose you've any news for me yet?' Pip asked, within five minutes of seeing her.

Leyne did not pretend not to know what she was talking about. 'It's a bit early yet, love. Er—it may take weeks rather than days,' she replied. With Max more or less incommunicado, she had not the first idea where to look. And supposing she were to find out. Did she have the right to tell Pip? Conversely, did she have the right to withhold that information from her? 'I'll be as quick as I can.'

'I know you will,' Pip said trustingly—and at the little girl's faith in her, so Leyne knew that she could just not ignore her need to know who her father was.

The trouble was, where to start? Pip was safely tucked up in bed that night when Leyne acknowledged that it had seemed no problem whatsoever to be appointed her niece's guardian. But Leyne could not help but feel like some petty criminal when, biting the bullet as it were, she that night quietly entered her sister's bedroom in search of Pip's birth certificate.

She supposed when she had located it that it had been too much to hope that the birth certificate of

Philippa Catherine Leyne might reveal who her father was. Leyne had been pretty certain, since her niece went by her mother's surname of Nicholson, that it would not show her father's name anyway. Even so, to see a short straight line in the space for 'Father' still came as a bit of a disappointment. All too clearly, Max did not want anyone to know the name of the father of her child.

Max had never spoken of him, and although Leyne supposed she must have had a natural curiosity at some stage, she was sensitive that some things were very private and were to be respected as such.

She put Pip's birth certificate away. It seemed Max's cellphone was permanently switched off, because all her attempts to reach her had come to nothing. Leyne briefly toyed again with the idea of using that emergency number and have someone try to find her in that vast country of Brazil.

But, in the end, she abandoned the notion. She had assured Max that she could cope with whatever cropped up. It would be like throwing in the towel at the first hurdle. It suddenly came to her that she must think not of what Max would want, but must think of what was best for Pip.

Leyne thought back to eleven and a half years ago, when Max had given birth to her precious child: Pip, with her astonishing mop of jet-black hair. Max had been living at home then, and in fact she had never lived anywhere else. So…

Suddenly Leyne saw a chink of light, saw what was now blindingly obvious. If Max had been going out with someone, and she was too choosy to give herself to just anybody, then of course he must have called at the house for her. Which meant her mother, their mother, must know him! Their mother must know the name of Pip's father, and all about him.

Feeling very much like telephoning her mother straight away, Leyne made herself go downstairs and think about it.

Perhaps, on second thoughts, with her quest so delicate, a personal visit to her mother would be a better idea. While Leyne knew that she was very much loved by their mother, she was also aware of the special bond between her mother and Max that had probably begun when, widowed young, Catherine Nicholson—as she had then been—had cleaved to her toddler daughter.

Yes, definitely her mother would know, Leyne decided, and got out of bed on Saturday morning reflecting that she would again try to phone Max, but if she could still not contact her that she would contact her parent.

While Leyne still felt very undecided, not sure if she should be doing what she was contemplating, her imagination took off as she pondered if there was some dark reason why Max had never mentioned Pip's father. Was he some kind of villain, some jailbird, some monster, that Max had never breathed a word of who he was? Perhaps, Leyne fretted, she would be doing Max a disservice if her sister did not want Pip to know the name of her father because he was a felon?

From what she knew of Max, though, and how, while occasionally dating, she had always been most circumspect about who she went out with, Leyne could not see her being involved with anyone who was not upright and honest.

More often than not Leyne took Pip and Alice swimming on a Saturday morning. Leyne decided not to alter that morning's arrangement. She would leave it until Pip went to Alice's for her sleepover and would then ring her mother in St Albans and ask if it was convenient if she drove up to see her.

The best-laid plans…she discovered, when Dianne Gardner rang to say she had been called away unexpectedly to an elderly aunt who had been taken ill.

'Would you mind very much if we put off the sleepover until next Saturday?' Dianne asked.

'Not at all,' Leyne replied, and offered, 'If it will help I can have Alice here with me until you get back. She can stay the night here to save you rushing back.'

Silence for a moment as Dianne thought it over before, 'Would you mind?' she asked gratefully. 'I wouldn't…'

'It will be a pleasure,' Leyne assured her.

She was having a coffee, watching while Pip and

Alice outraced each other in the swimming pool, when she belatedly remembered she was supposed to be seeing Keith Collins that night.

Oh, grief! Taking out her phone, and hoping she had remembered his number correctly—this was not the first time she had cancelled their arrangements—she pressed out the digits—and waited.

'Keith,' she said, when she recognised his voice. 'Leyne Rowberry.'

'I shall never forgive you if you're putting me off!' he stated, in a voice that wasn't over-brimming with good humour.

'Wouldn't dream of it,' she replied cheerfully. 'The thing is—er—I wondered if you'd rather come to my place for coffee?' And quickly, lest he got the wrong idea, 'I can promise you one of your favourite sumptuous feasts first.'

'You're breaking our date!' he exclaimed heavily, and for a moment Leyne wondered if she even liked him.

'I'm offering an alternative,' she answered, concentrating her thoughts on the nicer side of him that she had previously seen.

'Too late now for *me* to make alternative arrangements,' he said—as if she'd be gutted if he couldn't come!

'Your choice,' she offered. If he wanted to try and find a date elsewhere, good luck to him.

The evening was not a success. The meal, if not

exactly sumptuous, was good. But, since the girls had helped with the coconut and orange pudding, it seemed churlish not to let them stay and eat with them.

Keith appeared to be making an effort to be charming, but he was obviously not devastated when Pip asked if they could be excused and, armed with various nibbles, she and Alice raced off up the stairs.

Leyne went to the kitchen to make coffee and saw that Keith's good humour was surfacing when, on her return, he joined her on the sitting room sofa. 'Sugar?' she asked, quite aware that he was sitting unnecessarily close. She poured him a coffee and put a few inches of space between them when she got up to reach to the table for the sugar bowl.

'You really have the most extraordinarily lovely hair,' he murmured of her light-coloured hair, with its naturally lighter strands of blonde—sugar was all too plainly not his first priority.

'Cream or milk?' she offered.

'Cream,' he replied, and, looking into her large blue eyes, 'To go with your lovely complexion,' he said. And, taking the coffee from her, he placed it down on the low table in front of them and turned as though to take a hold of her. He got as far as, 'Leyne, beautiful Leyne…' when hoots of laughter wafted down through the floorboards overhead. 'Oh, for—!' he exclaimed impatiently. And, totally put off his stride, 'Can't those girls keep quiet?'

'Not for more than five minutes, I shouldn't wonder,' she replied equably.

'How long will they go on for?' he asked, sounding hopeful and disgruntled at one and the same time.

'I'd be very surprised if they settled down this side of midnight,' Leyne answered. 'It's a sleep-over,' she added. She felt sorry for him, even though his hopes for the way the evening would end had never coincided with hers.

She guessed, when shortly afterwards Keith left, that he would not be asking her out again. It was a pity; she liked him a lot of the time. She was not, however, heartbroken.

Dianne Gardner called for Alice around mid-morning the next day, and ten minutes later Leyne rang her mother and asked if it was convenient for her and Pip to drive up to see them. Catherine Rowberry had remarried four years ago, and had generously allowed her two daughters and grand-daughter to remain living in their old home when she had moved to Hertfordshire with her new husband.

'I'd love to see you,' Catherine answered warmly. 'Roland has had a heavy cold, but he's no longer infectious.'

'Is he up to visitors?' Leyne asked doubtfully. While sympathising with Roland, she was not wanting her niece to catch his cold, albeit Pip had not suffered an asthma attack in an absolute age.

'You probably won't see him. You know how it

is—well, perhaps you don't—but while women have colds, men, as dear as they are, have flu. Roland may say hello, then go and rest.'

'Fancy going to see Nanna?' Leyne asked Pip, and saw the lovely dark-haired child's eyes light up.

'It's ages, simply ages, since I last saw Suzie!' she exclaimed of Roland Webb's Labrador dog.

Suzie came in handy, in as much as while Pip played in the large garden with the dog, it gave Leyne the chance to have a private conversation with her mother. Roland had heroically made it to his feet to greet them when they arrived, but, as her mother had hinted he might, had retired for a 'lie-down'.

'Er—Mum,' Leyne said, after some minutes of wondering which way to bring up a subject that had an unspoken taboo attached.

Leyne's pensive expression was not lost on Catherine Webb. 'This sounds serious?' she observed.

Leyne looked at her still beautiful fifty-six-year-old parent and knew that there was only one way to say this. 'Pip wants to know who her father is,' she stated, but the minute the words were out she saw her mother mentally strapping on armour to defend her firstborn.

'Maxine intends to tell her when she's old enough,' her mother answered, a touch stiffly.

It heartened Leyne that her sister fully intended to tell her offspring of her father. But Leyne knew that she could not leave it there. 'Pip wants to know

now, Mum,' she said, and insisted, 'I think she's old enough now.'

'She'll forget all about it soon. It's only a whim,' Catherine reasoned.

'She's been wanting to know for some while now.'

'It will pass.'

Leyne did not want to badger her mother, who was already starting to show prickles in her protectiveness of her eldest daughter. 'I don't think she will,' she pressed on. And, knowing her mother had lived in the same house until after Pip had celebrated her seventh birthday, 'As tractable as Pip is, you know what she's like once she has set her mind to something.'

Catherine Webb looked exasperated and worried all at the same time. 'Maxine will want to tell her herself.'

'Max isn't here,' Leyne reminded her mother quietly. 'I've tried countless times to contact her, but her phone isn't ringing out. And while I have an emergency number for—'

'I wouldn't call this an emergency!' her mother cut in hurriedly. 'Pip will just have to wait.'

Love her mother though she did, Leyne felt very much like telling her that she was not the one who was guardian to the child; she was not the one who would look up occasionally from whatever she was doing to find Pip looking at her as though she was just bursting to ask how far she had got along with her enquiries.

'I don't think it *will* wait, Mum,' she stated seriously. 'I'm worried that it's preying on Pip's mind.' Leyne broke off to try another tack. 'You must have met her father?'

'No,' her mother promptly replied. 'I never met him.'

Which, since she had always known her parent to be incapable of telling a lie, was something of a body-blow to Leyne. 'You never—?' She broke off, something in her mother's expression seeming to tell her that her mother knew more than she was telling. 'But you do know who he is?' she pressed.

Her mother gave her cross look, but did concede, 'He never came into the house. And it was only a brief affair—over almost before it began.'

'But it was long enough for Max to fall in love with him?'

Catherine Webb's expression softened. 'Oh, yes,' she said. 'She loved him.' A faraway look was in her eyes. 'Then Maxine came home one night and shut herself in her room. When the next morning I asked her what was wrong—it was obvious she had been crying—she said she wouldn't be seeing him again. Nor did she. In fact she refused to so much as mention his name ever again.'

'You know his name, though?'

Her mother sighed and, after a silent tussle with herself, finally gave in. 'His name is John Dangerfield.'

John Dangerfield. Leyne rolled the name around in her head. But she knew she had never heard of him. 'Can you tell me anything more about him?'

'I know very little about him. As I said, I never met him. He rarely came to the house, and the few times he did Maxine would be on the lookout for his car and would dash out to him. Though…' Her mother hesitated, but only for a moment or two, and then stated, 'I expect you to use the information judiciously, Leyne. Pip is at a very vulnerable age.'

'I know it. It's why I *am* being very careful here. Anything you tell me I'll treat with the utmost care,' Leyne promised. 'But we have to bear in mind that Pip is likely to grow more and more anxious if I just try to fob her off. And you know yourself how her asthma can be triggered when she gets emotionally upset. I want to avoid anything that might bring on an attack.'

Catherine looked out of the window to where Pip was now seated on a wooden garden bench, quietly talking to Suzie. 'Poor scrap,' she said softly of her granddaughter, and confessed, 'I really don't know much more than his name, but, in all fairness, I suppose I must allow she has every right to know. John Dangerfield,' she revealed, 'is the chairman of a company called J. Dangerfield, Engineers.'

J. Dangerfield, Engineers? Leyne did not know

the company, but the company name prodded a tiny wisp of memory—as if she had heard or read something about them recently.

'Before you go charging in to tell Pip what I've told you,' her mother cautioned, 'I think it might be an idea to contact him first.'

'I wasn't thinking of contacting him at all!'

'Then I think you should.' And at Leyne's look of enquiry. 'An utter darling though Pip is most of the time, you know how intransigent she can be on the odd occasion.'

'That's true enough,' Leyne had to admit.

And her mother went on, 'If I know anything at all about my granddaughter, she is not going to want to leave it there.'

'Ah…' Leyne murmured. 'You… Oh, grief— you think she'll actually want to *meet* him?'

'Wouldn't you?'

Leyne thought about it, and had to acknowledge that she would not want to leave it at just knowing his name. Weakly, realising that she was taking on more than she possibly should, she was very tempted to leave matters until Max returned home. Leyne then made the mistake of glancing out of the window to where Pip was now looking back at her—with that direct kind of look on her face. And Leyne knew then that whatever it took to bring that little girl peace of mind she would do it. 'You're right, of course,' she admitted.

'Then I suggest you contact him first before you tell her who he is.'

'Oh, I don't—'

'Do it, Leyne!' her parent instructed sternly. 'Most definitely do it!'

'Why definitely?' she asked, unable to see why she should involve Pip's father at this stage.

'Because,' her mother replied firmly, 'for all we know he might want to deny paternity. He's never paid a penny towards Pip's upkeep after all. Not that Maxine would ever ask for his support; she's much too proud for that,' Catherine said with dignity, and Leyne did not have to wonder from where her sister, herself too for that matter, had inherited that pride.

She and Pip were on their way back to their home in Surrey when Leyne was again made to realise that Pip was every bit as bright as she had always thought. 'You and Nanna were having a good chat,' she remarked. 'Was it about me?' she asked, in her forthright manner.

Leyne saw no reason to lie to her. 'I thought Nanna might be able to tell me something about your father, and—'

'Did she?' Pip asked eagerly. 'Was—?'

'Oh, love, try to be patient. I know it's difficult for you, but it may take quite some while.'

Leyne hated not to be able to tell her what she had learned that day. And, had her mother not insisted she contact the chairman of J. Dangerfield, Engineers, before she acquainted Pip with her father's name, Leyne might well have said more. But, on thinking about it, Leyne knew that her mother was right and that her niece would not want to leave it there. She would fidget and fidget at it and would not rest until she had met him. Leyne blamed herself that she had not thought it that far through. Pip could be a dogged little miss when she set her mind on anything. And what was more important to her than knowing—and meeting—her father?

Leyne faced then that, having willingly volunteered to act as Pip's guardian, the task, up until Pip had asked that one important question, had been no task at all. But in her mother's absence she *was* the dear child's guardian, and therefore it was up to her, and no one else, to make whatever decisions were necessary in regard to the child's welfare. Decisions, no matter how difficult, which were not to be shirked.

With the company name J. Dangerfield, Engineers, to the forefront of her mind, and a certainty growing in her head that she had heard or read some snippet about that firm recently, Leyne had to wait until Pip was in bed before she could take any action.

As luck would have it, there were almost a week's newspapers awaiting collection for recycling.

After scouring three newspapers, Leyne was beginning to believe her memory for things inconsequential had let her down. But then, on the fourth paper, not in the business section, as she had supposed, she found herself staring at that which had stayed in her retentive brain for no particular reason.

It was a picture of one very good-looking, self-assured male, attending some gala evening. *Just good friends?* asked the caption, plainly referring to the glamorous and sophisticated-looking brunette hanging on his arm.

Jack Dangerfield, chairman of J. Dangerfield, Engineers, with his current lovely. Will Gina Sansome have more luck with the wily bachelor?

With her heart pounding Leyne studied the picture of the tall, dark-haired man. John Dangerfield, obviously known to all and sundry—with the exception of her mother—by the well-established diminutive form as Jack.

He was good-looking, far too good-looking for his own good in Leyne's opinion, and, by the sound of it, still unmarried. And that annoyed her—he was running around fancy-free while Max had had to make sacrifices here and there in order that their daughter should want for very little.

Reading on, Leyne thought he looked to be about the same age as Max, perhaps about a year or so older. Young, however, to be chairman of a problem-solving firm of engineers who apparently, so she read, had an international reputation. Well, all she hoped, Leyne mused, was that as well as solving safety engineering problems, he could safely help her solve this particular nearer to home non-engineering problem.

Wondering if the fact that he must have been extremely ambitious to head such a well-respected company at his mid-thirties age was the reason why—not wanting to be tied down—he and Max had parted company, Leyne went to where they kept the telephone directories.

J. Dangerfield, Engineers, had many business lines, she found, but, not knowing Jack Dangerfield's home address, it was plain she was going to have to contact him through his business.

Something, she discovered the very next morning, that was easier said than done. 'Can I help at all?' enquired the second person she spoke to.

'It's—er—a personal matter.'

'Just one moment.'

'May I help you?' enquired a third voice.

'I need to speak with Mr Jack Dangerfield. It's a private matter,' she added quickly, before she could be fobbed off.

She was fobbed off just the same. 'Mr Dangerfield is out of the office for most of this week. Perhaps if you wrote in?' suggested number three, which was of no help at all.

Feeling frustrated beyond measure, Leyne only

just managed to hang on to her manners. 'Thank you, I will,' she replied, and came away from the phone finding that she could be every bit as stubborn as the other females in her family when she had to be.

She penned the letter straight away.

Dear Mr Dangerfield,
I need to speak with you on an urgent matter of family business.

She was very tempted to add something to the effect that it was about time he woke up and, instead of squiring elegant females to social functions, devoted some time and attention to his daughter. But she wanted to see him herself first; wanted first to judge if, despite him looking affable enough in his picture, he might turn out to be someone she would not want Pip to have any contact with. So, having written just that brief note, she signed herself, 'Yours sincerely, Leyne Rowberry.'

And a fat lot of good it did her. A whole week went by, and—having decided not to give her mobile phone number or her office number—she did not want to take his call there but had written both her home phone number as well as her address—she had heard not a word from Mr Jack Dangerfield.

Pip had suffered a small asthma attack yesterday.

It had proved nothing to be too alarmed about. But Leyne was concerned, and could not help wondering if the sensitive child was getting herself in something of an emotional stew with regard to her unknown father. Leyne had checked her niece over carefully on Monday morning before deciding she was well enough to go to school.

Leyne waited until ten o'clock and then, regardless that she was at her office, she rang J. Dangerfield, Engineers. 'Mr Jack Dangerfield, please,' she said, her tone businesslike. And was put on to voice number two. Leyne dug her heels in. 'Mr Dangerfield *is* in today?' she enquired, in her best professional manner.

'He is. But he's very busy. If I could—'

That the man was in business that day was all Leyne needed to know. 'Thank you,' she cut in on number two, injecting a smile into her voice—and rang off. Next she rang Dianne Gardner. 'I have a bit of a problem,' she began.

'Anything I can help with?'

'I may be a bit late collecting Pip tonight,' she explained, hoping Dianne would think she was working late. 'Would it be any trouble for her to stay on with you until I can get there?'

'No trouble at all. Don't rush. She can have dinner with us,' Dianne offered. Their reciprocal back-up arrangement was working well.

Leyne went to see her boss just after lunch. 'I

need some time off. Is it all right with you if I work from home?'

Tad Ingleman sighed dramatically. 'It will be a dull afternoon without you,' he said, his eyes appreciative of her dainty features and shining hair. But, with the scheduled move to larger premises delayed yet again, 'If you can clear your desk before you go we can all spread out a bit.'

'I'll be in tomorrow,' she promised, and, armed with work she would have to catch up on that evening, she went to her car. Instead of heading home, though, she made for the offices of J. Dangerfield, Engineers.

Her telephone enquiry had yielded the information that Mr Dangerfield was in, but was busy. She smiled. No problem.

Glad that it was a non-rainy October day, Leyne parked her car and went and found herself a vantage point. Without doubt chairmen as busy as Jack Dangerfield appeared to be did not keep to nine-to-five hours. Though if he was going to work very late— and Leyne was prepared to stay there until midnight if need be—she would have to ring Dianne again.

That phone call, however, proved unnecessary when, at half past four, the main doors of J. Dangerfield, Engineers, opened and a man she instantly recognised from his newspaper picture came, briefcase in hand, out through the doors.

He was a fast mover, and was down the steps

before she had got over her surprise and budged an inch. Then she was galvanised into action. Fortunately he was heading her way.

'Mr Dangerfield!' She accosted him before they drew level.

His eyes flicked over her neat and curvaceous figure, taking in her lovely face and hair, and superb blue eyes. 'You have the advantage,' he paused to drawl charmingly.

'Leyne Rowberry,' she supplied, and looked into his eyes for a flicker of recognition at her name. There was none, but a small gasp of breath escaped her. Oh, my word, those eyes! There was no need to ask from where Pip had inherited her lovely green eyes. Nor too her jet-black hair. 'Er—I wrote to you.' She gathered herself back together to explain.

'You did?' He glanced at his watch, all too plainly a man in a hurry.

'You didn't reply.'

'And what did you write about, Miss Rowberry?' he enquired, everything about him telling her she had about five seconds before he strode off and left her standing there.

'It's a family matter,' she replied, adding for good measure, lest he thought the problem was solely hers, 'Your family.'

He did not like that. All too clearly, as a chilly expression came over his good-looking features, his family were sacrosanct. He made to move off.

There was no time to dress it up. 'To be more precise, I wrote to you because of your daughter!' she said quickly.

That stopped him dead in his tracks. 'My what?' he demanded, an expression of such total astonishment replacing his chilly look that Leyne had the most appalling sensation that he did not even know he *had* a daughter.

Immediately she discounted that notion. That couldn't be right—could it?

CHAPTER TWO

'I WROTE to you about your daughter,' Leyne repeated firmly, determined, as disbelief and total scepticism replaced his look of astonishment.

But it was that look, his seemingly genuine look of this being the first he had heard that he had a daughter, that caused Leyne to falter, that odd notion starting to grow and grow that he had not even known that Max had given birth to his child. And Leyne found herself asking, 'You *do* know that you have a daughter?' She was beginning to feel a shade awkward. If he had been entirely unaware of Pip's existence, Leyne realised she had just dropped something of a very big bombshell on him.

A few moments later, however, and she was feeling more infuriated than awkward when, 'You're an attractive woman, Miss—er—Rowberry,' he drawled. 'Not to say quite beautiful—in a good light,' he added mockingly. 'Which makes me positive that had I had the—hmm—pleasure—I would most certainly have remembered it.'

His meaning was obvious, and colour flared to her face. Embarrassment mingled with anger. 'Your daughter wants to know who you are—your name!' she flared. 'And if—'

'The hell she does!' he retorted. But, giving her a steady-eyed stare, 'You have a daughter old enough to make such a request?'

'I'm twenty-three…' Leyne began, and was at once impatient with herself and him. 'Pip, Philippa, is eleven and a half—twelve next April. She—'

'You're not her mother,' he stated, clearly wanting to know what any of this had to do with her.

'I'm her aunt. Max—Maxine, Pip's mother, is my sister.'

'Maxine Rowberry,' he said, chewing over the name before pronouncing, 'Never heard of her. Therefore, never met the lady.'

'Her name's not Rowberry; it's Nicholson.'

'Same applies,' he replied, plainly not even having to think about it. 'Mrs Nicholson?' he enquired.

'Miss,' Leyne enlightened him. 'Max is my half-sister. She isn't married.'

'Why hasn't she told the child who her father is?'

'Max always intended to, but—'

'Why didn't *she* write to me?' he questioned, a direct look in those green eyes.

Apart from those green eyes, who did that direct

look remind her of? No need to guess. 'My sister is abroad on business for six months. In her absence, I'm her daughter's guardian.'

'Hmph!' It seemed, as he gave another quick glance to his watch, that Jack Dangerfield had all the information he required. 'I'm late for my appointment,' he told her shortly, and appeared about to stride off.

'Mr Dangerfield!' She stopped him, her voice sharp in her moment of anxiety. 'I can't leave it like this! I—'

'I'm afraid you'll have to. If you've written to me your letter will be on file,' he stated. And, already on his way, 'My PA will contact you,' he added.

'But—' Leyne protested anyway—a totally wasted exercise. He was gone and she was speaking to herself.

Feeling door-slammingly frustrated, and not a scrap further forward, and doubting very much if she would be hearing from either Jack Dangerfield or his PA, Leyne went to her car and drove home.

When she had calmed down sufficiently she rang Dianne Gardner and explained she was home earlier than expected and would collect Pip shortly.

'No need if you've work to catch up on,' Dianne assured her, aware that Leyne quite often worked from home. 'The girls are fine, and, to tell the truth, having Pip here as her guest seems to bring out Alice's better manners.'

Realising she must be referring to the stroppy phase Dianne had told Max that Alice was going through, Leyne put down the phone and glanced at the work she would complete before morning.

She did not start work straight away, however, but thought back to her meeting with Jack Dangerfield. Though in actual fact it had been more a mutual ruffling up of antagonistic feathers than a meeting! Hardly a meeting either, since it had been none of his making but more his initial halting when she had planted herself full-square in front of him on that pavement.

Leyne was not ashamed of what she had done. It was he who should be ashamed. How dared he deny paternity of Pip? Notwithstanding that they both had the same raven-black hair, one only had to look into those same green eyes to see the resemblance.

How *could* he walk away? Just like that! While it seemed true that he'd had no idea of Pip's existence until she had told him of his daughter, to walk off the way he had was inexcusable.

Well, he needn't think he could fob her off with his condescending 'My PA will contact you'! She would give him a few days, a week at the most, and if she hadn't heard from him by next Monday she would again be waiting for him when he came out from J. Dangerfield, Engineers.

Leyne's resolve to do just that was stiffened when, on collecting Pip and apologising for altering their usual end-of-school-day arrangement, Pip gave her one of her serious looks.

'What was the hold-up?' she wanted to know. Oh, crumbs. Leyne glanced at her raven-haired niece, but before she could make any reply, Pip, taking a deep breath, was plunging on, 'Was it something to do with my father?'

'Oh, darling,' Leyne cried. That direct look was there in Pip's eyes again. How could she lie to her? 'I've—been making enquiries,' she answered.

'And?'

As she should have known, Pip would not leave it there. 'And I'm sorry, love, it's still going to take some while.'

'But you're a bit further forward?'

'Um—yes,' Leyne had to admit, and felt as guilty as the devil when a beaming smile broke over her niece's earnest expression.

'When you do find out who my father is, will you arrange for me to meet him?' she asked—and Leyne's heart sank.

She had no idea how long Pip had been nurturing a need to not only know who her father was but, as Pip's grandmother had said, would want to meet him too. But it seemed to Leyne then that the least she could do would be to prepare her for the fact that her father was trying to deny that he *was* her father.

Leyne pulled her to her and gave her a hug. 'You

have to be prepared for disappointment, darling,' she said gently.

'How?' Pip looked puzzled, clearly not under-standing.

'Beautiful though you are, sweetheart, he—um—may not want to meet you.'

Pip's answer was to break out into a huge grin. 'He will,' she said confidently. 'I know he will. I feel it. I—just—feel it.' Another huge grin, and, 'Would you like me to make you some coffee?'

Oh, heavens. Leyne wondered how the child could be so sure, feel so sure her father would want to meet her, when she had attained the age of eleven and he had never bothered to look her up. Pip was not to know that Jack Dangerfield had not—up until to-day—even known he had fathered a daughter, much less that he was denying even knowing her mother.

Not for the first time Leyne wished that her sister was home, so Max could make the delicate deci-sions that had to be made.

But, as though conjuring her up, Max rang that night. Though Leyne did not get to know it had been Max until it was too late.

Leyne was in the study at work, intent with com-plicated matter on her computer, when the phone rang. Absently she reached for it and then heard Pip call, 'I'll get it.' Leyne smiled. Her niece, on her way to bed, may have said 'bye' to her friend Alice only an hour ago, but they still had lots to say to each other.

Unusually, Pip was not on the phone for very long, but only a few minutes later came into the study. 'That was Mummy,' she said happily. And, as Leyne instinctively reached for the phone extension, 'She's gone,' Pip informed her. 'Mum said she was in a great hurry, so it was just a snatched call from the nearest landline before they went off again, and goodness knows when she will be able to ring again. She said sorry not to have rung before, but she couldn't ring us on her mobile because she lost it in the river. She said to give you her love and a hug and to tell you that the beast'—that would be Ben Turnbull, Leyne guessed—'has mellowed a bit, though wasn't too chuffed when she dropped some of his stuff in the river too.'

There was so much Leyne wanted to ask her sister, but it was too late now. 'Happy, chick?' she asked softly.

Pip nodded. 'I wanted to ask Mum about my father—but I couldn't,' she confessed. 'And then Mum said she had to charge off, and something about tribes and the Amazon, but that she just wanted to hear my lovely voice before she and her knight in tarnished armour tried to catch up on a slipped timetable.'

Pip went to bed elated that her mother had made contact, blissfully unaware of the agitation of her aunt's thoughts.

While Leyne realised that her sister's lost telephone explained why her phone had been unanswered each time she had tried to contact her, Leyne could not help but wish that Max had rung ten minutes later than she had. If she'd done that then Pip would have been in bed and Leyne would have been able to have some kind of a private conversation with her. A conversation where she could have asked her what she wanted her to do with regard to Pip wanting to know, and meet, her father.

Leyne realised that it was because Max had wanted a few snatched words with Pip before her daughter went to bed that she had rung at the time she had. And, recalling Pip's overjoyed face, Leyne felt mean that she would have preferred in this particular instance if Max had phoned at some other time. As it was, heaven alone knew when she would ring again.

Leyne's thoughts drifted to the man who, it was becoming more and more evident, had not been informed that he was a father. What had gone wrong between her sister and Jack Dangerfield Leyne had no clue, but perhaps he was lying. Remembering his astonishment, somehow Leyne did not think he was. Up until today he'd had absolutely no idea that his time with Max had resulted in a daughter.

A daughter he was trying to deny. Well, tough! It was about time he faced up to his responsibilities. The fact that, as chairman of J. Dangerfield, Engineers, he must be a very responsible person had nothing to do with it. Responsible in business he might be; the same could not be said for his private life!

Dianne Gardner was called away again early the next morning, and said she was likely to be away for a couple of days. She was worried because her ex-husband was too committed to have Alice with him, but Leyne assured her there was no need to worry and that she would be pleased to have Alice stay with them. Dropping the girls off at school on Tuesday, Leyne drove on to her office and delivered the work she had finished the previous evening. Explaining that she needed to work from home, she stuffed her briefcase with enough work to keep her busy for the next two days.

As it happened, it suited her very well to work from home. Should Jack Dangerfield's PA ring, she would be there to take the call.

That call did not come, and by Thursday Leyne had formed the opinion that this had gone on long enough! Only last evening she had glanced up and found Pip's eyes on her, silently asking the question, Is there any news yet?

Feeling uptight herself as she drove to her office, Leyne could only imagine how much worse it must be for her young niece. That being so, the minute she had the office to herself, she rang the offices of J. Dangerfield, Engineers, and went through the same procedure as before.

This time, though, when she heard voice number three, she changed it slightly. 'My name is Leyne Rowberry,' she said firmly. 'I would like to speak with Mr Dangerfield.'

'Just one moment, Miss Rowberry. I'll see if he's available,' the efficient-sounding voice answered to her surprise.

Leyne waited, fully expecting to be told that Mr Dangerfield was in Timbuktu, or somewhere equally unlikely, when, to her further surprise, the next voice she heard—was his!

'Miss Rowberry,' he said.

'Mr Dangerfield,' she replied, and was stumped for the moment by the realisation that she must have previously been talking to his PA, who must know something of her to have let her through her screening position.

'You rang me?' he reminded her when she had nothing to add.

'You were going to contact me!' she reminded him, hostility starting to enter her tone.

'I was?'

His PA had been going to, so he said. It was the same thing. 'Are you playing with me?' she demanded.

'Now, there's a thought,' he drawled. And while she was chewing on that, and at the same time striving for control—there was more at stake here than the personal antagonism she felt towards this man—his tone suddenly changed to be all tough businessman. 'You expect me to take you seriously?' he questioned shortly.

'Yes, I do!' she retorted bluntly. 'There is more here than you and me. I've a vulnerable eleven-year-old in my care who is daily hoping I can tell her who her father is!'

There was a pause, as though Jack Dangerfield was taking on board what she had just said. Then, his tone more reasonable, 'From my point of view, Miss Rowberry, I have told you as plainly as I know how that I am not the child's father. You, clearly, do not believe me. So why don't you tell me what makes you so convinced that I am?' He paused again, but only to come back to demand, 'You're trying to tell me that she carries my family's birthmark?'

'No, I'm not! Pip doesn't have a birthmark!'

'Which is in your favour—there isn't one.'

'Are you trying to trip me up?'

'You're trying to get me to admit to something that I *know* is untrue,' he reminded her. 'Again I ask—why are you so sure that I fathered the child?'

'I asked my mother.'

'Not the child's mother?'

'The child's name is Philippa! We call her Pip!' Leyne flared, feeling awkward suddenly, but starting to object to her niece being discussed as though she were a parcel. 'And I told you that her mother is out of the country and likely to be for some while. And that is why I asked my mother.'

'You were obviously too young when I was— er—sowing my wild oats, but you—'

'Look here, you!' Leyne erupted. 'My sister is not some—some scrubber. She is a responsible and a loving person. And she would not have gone with you for some—er—cheap thrill. You would have meant something to her, and I'm not having you talking as if—'

'So she told your mother I was the child's father?' He cut through her tirade.

Leyne counted to ten. 'Max did not have to tell her. You were the only man my sister was dating at the time!'

'I see,' he said, but was obviously just mulling over in his mind what Leyne had just told him. 'Then it seems to me,' he concluded, 'that I had better come and have a word with your mother.'

'What for?' All of Leyne's protective hackles rose up. 'My mother doesn't live with us. But, anyway, my mother has never met you.'

'I never called at your home for your sister?'

'You know you did! Only you never came into the house.'

'Did I never meet your father either?' He was starting to sound sceptical—as he had last Monday.

'I don't think so. It was around that time that my father fell ill—he died less than a year later.'

There was a brief pause, then Jack Dangerfield threw her completely with his next question. 'Who do you live with?' he wanted to know.

'Who…?' She just wasn't with him.

'You said you didn't live with your mother,' he replied patiently—as though she were the eleven-year-old under discussion. 'Are you living with someone—some man?'

'No!' she answered abruptly. 'It's just Pip and me, and Max when she's home. We live in the family home—my mother's home. She thought it best that we stayed put when she remarried four years ago.' Thanks to their mother allowing them to live there rent-free, they were able to cope financially most of the time. 'But this isn't getting anything settled and…'

'And I'm a busy man.'

He could run if he thought she was going to apologise for interrupting his day. 'So too am I busy!' she snapped.

'You work *and* look after the—Philippa?'

'It's no hardship, and I'm able to work from home when necessary,' she replied. And, as a sudden dreadful thought struck her, 'I'm not after your money!' she told him hurriedly. 'Please don't think that for a minute. Pip has everything she needs, I promise you. It's just that…' her voice softened '…that she's reached an age where her mind is starting to be more enquiring. And what she wants to know more than anything is who her father is.' Leyne gave a heartfelt sigh. 'It could not have come at a worse time.'

'I can see that,' Jack Dangerfield commented, and sounded as if he understood.

So much so that Leyne found she was telling him, 'Not only that, but Pip wants to meet him.'

Instantly Jack Dangerfield's tone changed. 'You can count me out on that one!' he rapped sharply.

'Trust me, I'd want to know a lot more about you before I let you within a mile of her!' Leyne retorted.

'Good!' he barked. But sounded a touch more polite when he enquired, 'So what is it you want from me, Miss Rowberry?'

'I want to be able to tell my niece the name of her father.'

'Can't you just tell her he died? That he fell off a cliff or something?'

'I'm not going to lie about something like that!' Leyne gasped, appalled at the very suggestion. But, realising belatedly that he probably already knew that, and was most likely just winding her up, 'You are just *not* taking this seriously,' she flared, starting to get furious with this man.

'Believe me, I find it very difficult to take any of this too seriously,' he shot back at her. And, before she could say another word, 'Tell me, where is your sister—correction, your half-sister—now?'

'I've told you. Abroad. She's a photographer. She's working all over on this trip.'

'She frequently travels overseas?'

'No,' Leyne admitted. 'This is her biggest opportunity. When she was asked to assist Ben Turnbull, Max—'

'She's with Ben Turnbull? She must be good,' Jack Dangerfield cut in, clearly having heard of him.

'She is. She said she wouldn't go at first. But neither Pip nor I would hear of that.'

'So she went—and left you to rear her child.'

'It's not like that!' Leyne flew, not liking the way he was making it sound as though Max was running out on her responsibilities. 'I've lived with and helped look after Pip since she was born. She's almost as much a part of me as she is my sister. It just isn't any problem taking care of her.'

'It sounds to me as though you *do* have a problem.'

Leyne bit her lip. 'We just hadn't anticipated that Pip would want to know—'

'If I'm reading this correctly,' Jack Dangerfield cut in, 'the child—Pip—is not going to be satisfied in meekly accepting any male name you pull out of the hat.'

'It's you!' Leyne erupted. 'It's your name, not just any man—'

'It seems to me,' he again cut in, ignoring her anger and sounding tough again, 'that you'd better contact your sister and get her to come clean about what she's been up to. It—'

'What kind of man are you?' Leyne exploded. 'If you had any decency at all, you'd—'

'It's because I do have a sense of decency that I'm bothering to speak to you now while my other calls are backing up,' he chopped her off curtly. 'As it is, I think I've given this—matter—far more time than could *decently* be expected of me. And now, if you'll excuse me, I'll—'

'Don't you dare put that phone down on me!' Leyne blazed, knowing he was about to do just that. 'I don't know what went wrong between you and Max that makes you so determined to deny paternity, and I don't want to know, but—'

'I'm a busy man, Miss Rowberry.' He unapologetically interrupted her furious flow. 'I'll call and see you in my free time.'

'No, you won't!' she erupted, panic-stricken for the moment.

'I'll phone you first,' he informed her, and, whether she liked it or whether she didn't—and she didn't—he terminated the call.

For several minutes afterwards no name was too bad for him. But as her fury subsided she wondered if he meant what he'd said and would call and see her. Fear that he might come face-to-face with Pip began to surge upward, but then Leyne comprehended that by saying he would phone first Jack Dangerfield meant that he would take jolly good care that Pip was not around when he called.

Admitting to feeling very frustrated by the whole business, Leyne began to ponder what she had hoped to get from her phone call to him anyway. She was not yet ready for him and Pip to meet, so supposed that, while wanting him to admit to being Pip's father, she had also wanted to let off steam that neither he—nor his PA—had been in touch.

Keith Collins stepping into her office and asking her out momentarily took thoughts of Jack Dangerfield from her mind. Keith was at his charming best, reminding Leyne of why she liked him. 'I thought you'd had enough,' she answered with a grin.

'I haven't begun to have nearly enough yet,' he replied, adopting a lecherous look.

Leyne had to laugh. 'As it happens, I'm fairly sure I can be free tomorrow night,' she accepted, and later phoned Dianne to ask if she could drop Pip off on her way out.

Dianne was only too willing, and Leyne began to look forward to an evening out with Keith. As it would be a Friday, with no school the next day, it would not matter if Pip was late going to bed.

As usual Leyne checked for telephone messages as soon as they arrived home, but telephone messages there were none. Nor did Jack Dangerfield phone that evening. And by morning, as she did the school run with Pip and Alice, Leyne was starting to get cross that she had obviously been fobbed off yet again.

The light of battle entered her eyes when there was no message left on the phone when she arrived home that evening. But she had neither Jack Dangerfield's home phone number nor his home address, and there was nothing she could do about it until Monday.

Keith Collins did not appear entirely ecstatic when he learned that his evening with Leyne was going to end well before midnight. But, like the normally nice person she thought he was, he appeared to have accepted that if he wanted to date her, it had to be on her terms.

All of which made her warm to him as they dropped her niece off at Dianne's house and drove on to the eating establishment he had chosen.

Leyne enjoyed her meal, and enjoyed his company. She enjoyed too, because they would soon be picking up Pip, his kiss in the restaurant car park.

'Are you sure you haven't time to come back to my place for coffee?' he asked warmly.

Time to back away. 'I'm sure,' she replied pleasantly, and moved towards his car.

She was up early the next morning. Pip always got her swimming gear together herself, but Leyne always liked to check she had everything. Having just driven her car out of the garage, she had just closed the garage doors when Pip came out and said that Alice's mother was on the phone. Returning to the house, Leyne went to have a word with Dianne.

'Would you mind if I took the girls this morning?' Dianne asked. And in a quieter tone—so little ears must have been about, 'Alice is keen to show me how many lengths of the pool she can swim, and I get the impression that I'll be the most heartless mother in the world if I don't go along.'

Leyne said she did not mind one little bit, and, with the whole morning free once she had waved Pip goodbye, Leyne got out the vacuum cleaner and set about a chore she did not care very much for but, since she could not live in an unkempt house, was a necessary one.

She had just switched the machine off, however, when the telephone rang. Max? Leyne made a dive for it. 'Jack Dangerfield,' said a voice she was beginning to recognise, and for a moment she did not know if she was glad or sorry it was him.

'Good of you to ring,' she said, none too prettily.

'I said I would,' he replied urbanely. 'I can be with you shortly if it's convenient?'

About to abruptly tell him he was lucky to find her in, she halted. She was the instigator here. And by 'convenient' he meant if Pip was not around. 'As it happens Pip will be out until around twelve-thirty,' Leyne informed him, and did not have to say more apparently, because the line went dead.

And that niggled her. How soon was shortly, for goodness' sake? He knew where they lived from her letter, obviously, but not a word of enquiry as to how to find her address.

A second or two later she was realising that, as opposed to her car, which was creakily on its last legs, he probably had an up-to-the-minute car that included satellite navigation amongst its many refinements. All he had to do was to key in the postcode she had written and he would be on his way. Though a few seconds after that and she was calling herself all sorts of an idiot. Of course he knew the address. He had driven a car to this address some twelve years or so before—to call for Max!

Jack Dangerfield certainly hadn't had any difficulty finding their home anyway, as was proved when, not much more than five minutes later, barely giving her time to do more than put the vacuum cleaner away, Leyne saw a smart black car pull up on the drive and park behind her car. She owned to experiencing a flurry of activity in her insides—she wasn't ready to see him.

She found a need to check on her appearance, and quickly dived into the downstairs cloakroom. The mirror there showed her long fair hair pulled back from her face, and large blue eyes looking back. Leyne had a hand up, ready to take the band from her hair before—for goodness' sake, she fumed impatiently—the doorbell sounded and she went to answer it with her hair left as it had been.

'You found us all right,' she murmured, remembering her manners as she invited him into her home. He ignored her sociable enquiry. She wondered why she had bothered. 'Come into the sitting room,' she said, polite still, and led the way. 'Would you like coffee?' she stayed polite to enquire civilly.

He shook his head. 'I want to be away long before twelve-thirty,' he replied succinctly.

Well, he needn't bother. She wanted him out of her home long before Dianne dropped Pip off. Determined to stay civilised, Leyne took a seat on one of the several easy chairs in the room, and relaxed a little when he followed suit. Jack Dangerfield was tall, and somehow, even sitting down, he still seemed to dominate the room.

Leyne was staring at his jet-back hair, her gaze flitting to his eyes, green, and identical to those of her niece, when he interrupted her inventory. 'Your niece is out somewhere, you said?'

Quickly Leyne gathered herself together. 'She and her friend Alice more often than not swim on a Saturday morning,' she replied. And, lest he should think his daughter neglected in any way— for all he had not yet admitted to being Pip's father, 'Dianne, Alice's mother, and I have an arrangement where one or other of us does the ferrying around. Dianne will keep an eye on the girls this morning.'

She could have saved herself the breath, Leyne

realised—he was not the least bit interested. 'You're still insisting that I'm the child's father?'

That same raven hair! Those same green eyes! Add that to what her mother had told her. 'There's no doubt about it in my mind,' she answered firmly.

Jack Dangerfield favoured her with an impatient look. Clearly he did not want a daughter foisted on him, particularly a daughter he had never known about. 'Her mother's abroad?' he questioned.

She had already told him that! 'South America at the moment,' Leyne informed him.

'I thought you said she was in Australia,' he threw her by stating.

Leyne blinked—where had Australia come from? 'No, I didn't!' she replied sharply.

He did not seem convinced. 'But she has been to Australia?' he pressed.

'Max has never *been* to Australia,' Leyne told him bluntly. 'It may be on their itinerary before she comes home, hopefully in time for Pip's next birthday, but it will be Max's first visit there.'

He shrugged, but accepted what she said. 'I must have been thinking of someone else.'

'No doubt,' Leyne replied. She would not be at all surprised if he had many ex-women-friends in all corners of the globe.

'Well, I have to tell you, Miss Rowberry—' he

began, and looked so serious that she stared at him from her wide blue eyes, expecting some quite shattering announcement. But as he stared back—his eyes on her eyes and on the earnest look of her—he checked. And, after a moment when—ridiculously, she later thought—time seemed suspended, he merely added, 'That I—hmm—would like to take up your offer of coffee after all.'

Leyne went to the kitchen and could not help feeling a little let down. Though quite what she had been expecting him to say she wasn't sure. He seemed determined not to acknowledge Pip as his—and Leyne was not at all certain what she could do about that.

She returned to the sitting room with a tray of coffee, knowing that for her niece's sake, and no other, she must be equally determined.

'Oh, if only Max had not lost her cellphone.' She mumbled her thoughts out loud as she handed him his coffee and took her coffee back to the chair she had been seated in a short while ago.

'Cellphone?' Jack enquired politely.

'I can't even contact her—not unless it's a real emergency. Max has so much equipment to carry, her mobile phone came to grief and landed in some river,' Leyne explained.

'Otherwise you'd ring her for the full low-down?'

Leyne tossed him a peeved look. 'I'd ring her for guidance. I just *know* that you are Pip's father,' she said heavily, going on weightily, 'Forgive me for being blunt, but, while I can easily believe that the—er—male of the species could quite casually—er—bed some female and then forget totally about her—'

'Too kind,' Jack interrupted her coolly.

'Max is just not like that.' Leyne, feeling hot about the ears, ploughed on. 'My sister just isn't promiscuous, and never has been.'

'Which is why you feel you can, so casually, pin the fatherhood charge on me?'

'I know it's you. My mother—'

'You want concrete proof?' he interrupted again. 'I'll give you concrete proof.'

'How?' Suddenly Leyne was feeling wary.

'There's one very simple way to prove I am not the child's father.'

'And that is?' Leyne questioned, her eyes fixed on his.

His steady-eyed gaze held hers. 'You're obviously not going to believe me whatever I tell you,' he commented. 'But I guess even you would trust a DNA test.'

That well and truly took the wind from her sails. He was prepared to take a DNA test? Her mouth fell a little way open. She closed it as she thought of Pip.

'No!' Leyne told him.

'You wouldn't trust a DNA test?' he asked, his eyebrows ascending.

'Yes, I would. But I don't want to go that route.'

'You've changed your mind? You're now ready to believe me? To believe I am not the—?'

'I'm saying nothing of the kind!'

'Then it seems to me it's put your money where your mouth is time. Though naturally I would pay any expenses involved. Either we settle this once and for all with a test or—'

'I don't want Pip upset!'

'You haven't told her that I'm her father?' he questioned sharply.

'Of course I haven't!' Leyne retorted.

'Then you must be saying that—now I've shown you a way of proving you've got the wrong man— you've changed your mind. That you know in advance it's not me.'

'No, I'm not!' Leyne erupted hotly. 'Pip is a sensitive eleven-and-a-half-year-old with a small asthma problem. What I'm saying is that I don't want her upset or involved in anything sordid.'

'Sordid?' he challenged toughly.

'Pip is very bright. If she has to have a blood test, she is intelligent enough to want to know why.'

Jack Dangerfield took that in, and suddenly his tough attitude softened.

'It doesn't have to be a blood test,' he pointed out.

'A mouth swab would still make her ask questions,' Leyne argued.

He gave her that direct look she knew so well—

her niece had an identical look. There was no mistake about it—he *was* Pip's father. But he was looking tough again when, sounding fed up at being messed about, he arrogantly clipped, 'The floor is yours, Miss Rowberry.'

'I suppose,' Leyne conceded reluctantly, not feeling very happy about what she felt forced to propose, 'that I could raid her hairbrush.' He was giving her that direct look. 'Perhaps there will be enough DNA there to prove what I know is the truth,' she felt compelled to go on, yet it did not seem quite the thing to her, to raid her niece's hairbrush—but needs must when the devil drives. And with this particular devil so determined that he was not Pip's father, something had to be done.

Then all at once Leyne began to feel troubled by the ethics of what she was doing. Against that, though, what value ethics when weighed against the inner fretfulness, the extent of which she could only guess, that Pip was going through? A moment later and Leyne could not bear that Pip should have this anxiety gnawing away at her. The matter had to be resolved, and soon.

'As it happens, Pip is at an age where brushing and experimenting with her long hair is quite a fad.' Leyne took a deep breath and, there being no other way, 'If you'll excuse me,' she said primly, and left the room.

Upstairs in her niece's room, Leyne was glad that Pip had a different, wider-pronged hairbrush that she took when she went swimming, and always left her other hairbrush behind.

As anticipated, her hairbrush had more than sufficient hair to satisfy any DNA scientist. Leyne carefully gleaned all hair from it, having some idea, rightly or wrongly, that it was the hair roots that mattered.

For good measure she went to the bathroom and, as she did every so often, replaced Pip's toothbrush with a new one. From there Leyne went to the kitchen and found a couple of small bags to put her finds in.

'I've included her toothbrush,' Leyne said on returning to the sitting room. 'I don't know if the DNA has been rinsed away—probably it has. But you never know.'

With that she handed over the two bags. Jack Dangerfield, already on his feet, took both bags from her, but opened neither. A pity, Leyne thought. Had he done so he would have seen in one of them an identical match for his own jet-black hair.

'I'll be in touch,' he said, and was halfway to the door when a car pulled up outside.

Leyne went to the sitting room window and immediately recognised the car. It was Dianne Gardner's car! Even with the evidence of two cars on the drive Dianne peered to see her, to check that she was home. Then turned to say something to Pip, who got out.

'Oh, no!' Leyne said faintly, as Dianne drove away. Leyne had not wanted Jack Dangerfield and

Pip to meet, but there, racing up the drive, her raven-black hair flying out behind her, her swimming bag slung over her shoulder, was her niece. 'She's early,' she said on a whisper of sound.

'Philippa?' the man by her side questioned.

'Philippa,' Leyne answered. 'Pip.'

CHAPTER THREE

LEYNE had still not fully collected her thoughts when Jack Dangerfield pocketed the two bags she had given him and Pip, aware from the strange car on the drive that her aunt had a visitor, came looking for her.

'You're early,' Leyne said with a smile, glad to hear she was sounding much more calm than she felt.

'Alice had an accident,' Pip replied, staring at the visitor as if fascinated.

'What happened?' Leyne asked. She wasn't anywhere near ready for the tall man staring down at the raven-haired child with some kind of watchful interest to meet the full curiosity of her niece. 'Is Alice badly hurt?'

'She did a wonky dive and hurt her wrist, but she was really, really brave,' Pip reported. 'Her mum gave her a bit of a telling off—there's a notice that says no diving in the shallow end…' she explained, but, her voice tailing off, she studied the man with whom she shared the same colour hair and eyes.

'Mrs Gardner dropped me off on her way to the hospital—she thinks Alice may have sprained her wrist,' Pip ended and, giving her full concentration to the man who was looking intently back at her, 'Hello,' she said shyly.

'This is Mr Dangerfield.' Leyne came alive to perform the introductions.

Jack Dangerfield had clearly not missed that the young girl had the same raven hair and the same coloured eyes. But his voice betrayed nothing of his thoughts as, before Leyne could complete the introduction, 'You must be Philippa,' he said.

Green eyes looked into green eyes. 'Everybody calls me Pip,' she told him solemnly. But as he continued to observe her, and she him, a flush of colour all at once stained her sweet unblemished skin. And, her eyes fixed on him as though hypnotised, she abruptly blurted out, 'My mother's a photographer.' And, in her sometimes forthright manner, 'Do you know her?' she asked.

Leyne only just held back a sharp pull of breath. If Jack Dangerfield had not noted the two characteristics they shared, then Pip unquestionably had. Instinctively Leyne stretched out a protective arm and drew her niece to her side—an action not lost on him.

But Leyne did not know whether to be glad or sorry when, putting an end to any speculative thoughts the child may have, he replied, quite kindly, Leyne later realised, 'No, Pip, I have never met your mother.' And, with a warm smile that Leyne felt would have charmed birds out of trees, 'But I'm very pleased to have met her daughter.'

Pip blushed again, but, either overcome by disappointment or shyness, said not another word; Leyne, rescuing the situation as best she could, smiled as she addressed the man who—if he was not Pip's father, and Leyne was sure he was—had just put a stop to any flight of fancy the child might have. 'I'll show you out,' she said pleasantly.

'Thank you for the coffee,' he replied, equally pleasantly. Leyne let go her protective hold of Pip. 'Bye,' he courteously bade the young girl of whom he had just denied parentage.

'Bye,' Pip managed.

'She's bright,' he murmured when they were at the outer door and out of earshot.

'I told you she was.'

He opened the door. 'I'll be in touch,' he said, and did not wait for an answer. Neither did Leyne wait to see him drive away. She closed the door after him and hurried back to the sitting room.

'I thought it was him!' Pip mourned sadly. Her aunt did not go in for casual gentlemen callers and she had sensed that he was somebody special.

'Oh, darling, I know it's difficult, but please try to be patient a little while longer,' Leyne said softly, giving her a hug, not pretending not to know what she was talking about. 'I'm—still working on it. Now, what's this about Alice?'

Only when Pip was safely tucked up in bed that night did Leyne have space to go over the events of that day. Dianne Gardner had called in on the way home from the hospital and explained that she had feared worse than a sprained wrist but, although Alice had been diagnosed with a mild sprain, thankfully nothing was broken.

More to take Pip's mind off that which Leyne was fairly sure played a large part in her thoughts, Leyne had offered to take both girls shopping. 'Pip could do with some new shoes, and—'

'Oh, yes,' both girls had cried, and both Leyne and Dianne had had to smile.

Choosing exactly the right pair of shoes had taken for ever, but Pip had returned home happy, and Alice, who had spent some of the money her father had given her on her last visit on a new top, had—apart from the bandage on her wrist and a few moans— mainly forgotten about the morning's *contretemps*.

Keith had telephoned early that evening to see if she was free. She was not. But it was not thoughts of Keith that occupied Leyne as she mulled over Jack Dangerfield's visit.

He was adamant that he was not Pip's father. And, Leyne supposed, were that true, then he had done the only thing possible in straight away telling Pip that he had never met her mother. And Leyne supposed too that, since he must have realised what had been behind Pip's question of, 'Do you know her?' he had attempted to soften what might have been a painful reply, by adding that charming, 'But I'm very pleased to have met her daughter'.

But he *was*. Pip's father. Leyne knew it! She trusted her mother implicitly. And while she found it hard to believe that Jack Dangerfield had forgotten his relationship with Max, no matter how brief that relationship had been, and even if twelve years had elapsed since then, Leyne felt sure that he *must* know too that he was Pip's father.

So what did he hope to gain by having his DNA matched against Pip's? Apart from anything else— Max not being in the habit of sleeping around—he had only to look at Pip to know that she was his daughter. Those same striking green eyes, not to mention that jet-black hair.

Leyne had no idea how long it took to test DNA but, suspecting it would be a week or so, perhaps a little longer since it was being done by a hair sample and not a blood sample—which for some reason she felt would have been easier—she strove hard to be patient as she waited for his phone call.

As the days went by, however, with no call from Jack Dangerfield, she began to wonder if indeed he *would* call. And, as more days went by, if he did call, could she trust him to say if he and Pip were proved to be *not* related?

Well, if he thought she would believe it without inspecting the result for herself, he could think again! And if he wouldn't show her the paperwork she would jolly well have her own test taken. Though how she was going to get a hold of his hairbrush if he didn't intend to co-operate, she was uncertain.

As well as waiting for Jack Dangerfield to phone, Leyne was also hoping that her sister was in an area where she would make contact. It would all be so much simpler if she were able to ask Max personally if she had her approval to tell Pip that Mr Dangerfield did actually know her mother and was, in fact, her father.

But Max did not phone, and neither did the head of J. Dangerfield, Engineers. Max had said at the outset that she would keep in touch whenever she could, and that they were not to worry if she was unable to make contact. But Leyne was still anxious that her sister should phone. She was equally anxious too that Jack Dangerfield should ring.

When three weeks went by, and not one syllable did she hear from him, Leyne went from anxious to angry, and from angry to fuming. It was not good enough; it just wasn't! It was all right for him. He did not have to daily face the serious green eyes of an eleven-and-a-half-year-old silently asking that question, Who is my father?

During those three weeks Leyne had had several telephone conversations with her mother, and her mother, apprised of the details, counselled patience. But, with Pip's questioning eyes on her so many times, Leyne's patience was fast beginning to fade. She had been out with Keith Collins a couple of times, but only to come home and dash to see if there were any telephone messages. But on neither occasion had either Max or Jack Dangerfield rung.

Leyne had a date with Keith again that night. She was frequently asked out by other men of her acquaintance, but supposed she must like Keith most that at the moment he was the man she was dating. She had not told him that Pip was sleeping over at Alice's that night—and he hadn't bothered to ask about her child-sitting arrangements; if he thought that Pip was home, he would not expect to be invited back for coffee.

He was far from her mind, though, that Saturday as she drove Pip and her overnight bag round to her best friend's house. On Leyne's mind, as she drove back home to get ready for the evening, was one tall, green-eyed, black-haired man. She felt she had waited long enough.

First thing on Monday morning—well, as soon as his office was open—she was going to telephone him. And, if he refused to take her call, she would personally present herself at J. Dangerfield, Engineers, and waylay him as she had before. Though she had gone beyond wondering how she was going to get a sample of his hair for DNA testing. By then

Leyne was feeling furious enough with him to want to yank handfuls of his hair out by the roots. She doubted she would be feeling any less silently fuming come Monday.

As she let herself back into the house Leyne was even rehearsing, well in advance, a few of the choice things she was going to say to him. The ringing of the phone cut her off mid-snarl. She made a dive for the phone. 'Hello?' she said, on picking it up, her heart thumping. Max? Jack Dangerfield?

'Leyne?'

Leyne! What had happened to Miss Rowberry? She wasn't complaining, nor snarling—there were bigger issues here. Time to get snarly if he tried to put her off.

'Jack?' she said. She had no idea what sort of in-law relationship she had with him if he was about to confirm he was her niece's father, but, for Pip's sake, she must try to keep it friendly.

'How are you?' he enquired pleasantly.

How was she? Starting to get a little cross, if he must know! 'You've got the result back?' she asked, doing away with any pleasantries he may have in mind and getting straight down to priority matters.

There was a moment's pause before, 'I think we should meet,' he stated.

Leyne allowed herself a small smile of relief. That was positive. He obviously was not denying paternity any longer. Her smile faded. Well, not straight out, he wasn't. Perhaps he was intending to soften the blow.

Like blazes! She wasn't having that! 'Why?' she asked, a shade belligerently she had to admit. 'Why can't you—?'

'Where's Pip?' he cut her off.

Leyne did not thank him that plainly he did not want young ears around while they discussed this matter. 'You can talk,' she invited. 'Pip isn't here.'

'She's out somewhere?'

Suddenly he wanted to behave like a responsible parent? Encouraging! 'She's having a sleepover.'

'With her friend Alice?'

'It's what girls do.'

Silence for a second or so. 'Then you're free?' he asked. 'To have dinner with me?'

Her eyes shot wide in amazement. 'Actually, and strange as it may seem, I have a date this evening.'

Like he cared. 'I'll pick you up in an hour,' he said—and left her staring at a dead telephone.

Leyne was flabbergasted. 'I'll pick you up...' And furious! Even when she'd told him she had got a date! He could go— Leyne broke off mid-rant. He was not asking her out on a *date* date. 'I think we should meet,' he had said at the start, so clearly he had something to tell her. So why, once he had established that Pip was not likely to overhear any reaction her aunt had to anything he said, couldn't he have told her what he had to over the phone? All he'd had to say was, I have concrete proof that I am Pip's father. That was all he'd needed to say.

But, reluctantly accepting that she supposed she would need to talk over with Jack Dangerfield how he would want to tell Pip that he did in fact know her mother—quite well, too, as had been proven— Leyne picked up the phone and dialled Keith's number. He was going to love her!

'Keith…' she began when he answered. Five minutes later she put down the phone, fully aware that Keith was not the happiest ferret in the rabbit warren.

Not seeing why she should have to dine with Jack Dangerfield, Leyne went upstairs for a quick shower and to change. If he was hungry she could have given him something to eat here.

Though, on reflection, perhaps home was too intimate. Perhaps Dangerfield wanted what he had to say to be said on neutral ground. Leyne did not like the sound of that. Her mother was not some muddle-headed old lady. She was fifty-six, clear-sighted, and sharp with it—and Leyne had never, ever known her tell an untruth. If she said John Dangerfield, chairman of J. Dangerfield, Engineers, was the father of her daughter's child then it was for certain that he was. And Leyne would take a whole lot of convincing before she would believe otherwise.

Wearing a smart pair of trousers and a silk-lined very feminine georgette top, Leyne was only just ready when Jack Dangerfield pulled up on the drive.

She went to the door, mentally squaring her shoulders. Just let him deny it and she would demand to read that DNA result herself.

'You're ready!' He seemed surprised.

Good. She wouldn't want him to think she had made a special effort on his behalf. 'And waiting,' she answered lightly, and went to his car with him.

'You were able to cancel your date?' he enquired politely as they drove along.

As if he cared! 'Keith knows I'm not as—um—free as most single women. That—er—I sometimes have difficulty in making—' Leyne broke off. 'I'm not complaining. I wouldn't have it any other way.'

'So this Keith—he's a regular boyfriend?' Jack asked, ignoring her explanation.

She wondered why she was bothering to explain—it was he, Dangerfield, who had caused the complications to her evening's arrangements. Regular boyfriend? 'I suppose so,' she acknowledged—well, she wasn't dating anyone else at the moment.

'In love with him?' he asked.

Leyne turned to stare at him in surprise. What on earth did he think it had to do with him? 'What about you?' she enquired. 'Did you have to break a date in order to be free tonight? Is she your regular girlfriend—and are you in love with her?'

His answer was to laugh. She could have punched him. 'You're a fiery little thing, aren't you?' he observed, amused.

Leyne turned crossly to face the front and decided that she was going to ignore anything he said that was not to do with Pip and that DNA test.

Worried he wasn't, but he had done with small talk, apparently. And it was not until they were seated in the pleasant restaurant he had chosen that she felt the time had come for them to get down to one very important discussion.

'You—' she began, suddenly realising that she felt quite nervous about the outcome of this meeting. So much depended upon it for her lovely Pip and her anxious little mind.

'You've not heard from your half-sister recently?' Jack Dangerfield spoke over what she had been about to ask.

'No, I keep hoping that she'll make contact, but…'

'Hoping?' he picked up.

'Well, yes, of course hoping. Whatever I tell Pip is going to be pretty momentous for her. I would much prefer I had her mother's permission to go the route I'm going with this.'

'You think she will disapprove?'

'No, I don't think that. Max will know that I'll deal with this in the most sensitive way I can. And she did tell our mother that she had always intended to tell Pip about her father when she was old enough. I would just prefer that I had a word with Max first.'

'But she did appoint you legal guardian before she left?' he insisted.

'Well, not in front of lawyers. But in writing. You never know, I might need to sign permission should some medical or surgical emergency occur, and then—' Leyne broke off—they were getting away from the point. 'Yes,' she said bluntly. 'In her mother's absence, I am Pip's sole guardian. And, as such, I think I have every right to know the result of that DNA test. Presumably, by now, you do have the result?' Leyne pressed. He must have it. What was the point of her having dinner with him otherwise?

Leyne looked into his green eyes, her expression serious as she waited for him to answer. Oddly, though, when he had the same direct manner as her niece, he seemed to be taking his time, seemed to be weighing up what he had to say before he said it.

'Well?' Leyne persisted, starting to get more than a little impatient.

'It's—hmm—more complicated than I at first believed,' he said, when quite a few seconds had laboriously ticked by.

'How?' Leyne questioned shortly. 'Weren't the hair samples sufficient?'

He exhaled deeply. 'They did not prove that I'm the child's father. But,' he went on when Leyne stared at him in disbelief, 'there is sufficient evidence to show a blood relationship of some kind between Philippa and me.' And, having admitted that, 'But—'

'So you *are* her father!' Leyne cut in. 'For—'

'Not proven!' He cut her off this time.

It staggered Leyne that even with his DNA and the DNA from Pip showing that they were related in some way, he was still refusing to acknowledge that Pip was his daughter. For herself, Leyne would have walked out on him there and then. But she squashed the mighty impulse, again reminding herself that this was not for her, it was for Pip.

So, taking a deep and, she hoped, calming breath, Leyne tried another tack. 'My mother,' she began, 'does not, repeat *not*, tell lies. She would not have told me what she did had she not fully, *one hundred per cent*, believed it. And she,' Leyne went on severely, 'told me that the father of Max's baby is John Dangerfield, chairman of J. Dangerfield, Engineers.' Leyne observed that he looked a touch taken aback by what she had just said. Perhaps she had been a little fierce, but there was a serious issue here. 'So you tell me straight,' she ploughed on determinedly. 'Are you or are you not John Dangerfield, chairman of J. Dangerfield, Engineers?'

For several long seconds, saying nothing, he just sat and stared at her. Serious green eyes stared into stormy-looking big blue eyes. And then suddenly he gave her a smile of such extraordinary charm that her heart picked up a giddy beat. And that charm all about him, 'My friends,' he said softly, 'call me Jack.'

She had once, not very long ago, in fact, called

him Jack. Quickly, though, realising she was in danger of being swamped by his charm, Leyne gathered herself together. 'You're not willing to admit it, Mr Dangerfield?' She was determined that he should know she would never regard him as a friend. 'Even with the evidence you have that you and Pip share a blood relationship, you're still insisting that you are not her father?'

'The evidence is inconclusive,' he returned sharply. 'And, while I have to accept the blood tie, I will not have that child believing that I am her father.'

Leyne stared at him, her heartbeats back to normal. She was no longer hungry. She hoped he enjoyed his dinner. 'There seems little more to be said,' she informed him woodenly, and pulled back from the table. She knew that she needed time to think about this. About where did she go from here?

Jack Dangerfield's arm snaking out, his hand on her arm, stayed her, and stopped her from getting up and walking out of there. She looked at him coldly. 'Don't go,' he urged. 'There's more to be said.'

'There is?' she queried stiffly.

'Of course there is,' he retorted, letting go her arm, sounding so disbelieving that she could not see that, that Leyne found she was pulling her chair to the table once more.

'So?'

'Let's eat,' he said, as the waiter arrived with their order.

Leyne discovered she had more of an appetite than she had thought, and started on her Dover sole. 'You were saying?' she hinted between mouthfuls.

'I was saying,' he took up, 'that, having discovered my blood links to the child—Pip,' he corrected at Leyne's frosty look, 'I do not now intend to abandon her.'

Big of him! 'But you are not yet ready to acknowledge that you are her parent?'

'Tell me,' he asked, totally ignoring her question, 'what time will Pip be back home tomorrow?'

'Around eleven in the morning,' Leyne answered. 'Why?' she asked warily.

'Because,' he said, reading her body language, 'I would like to take her out to tea.'

'No! Oh, no!' Leyne told him point-blank.

'Why not?' he questioned.

'I won't allow it,' she replied promptly.

'*You* won't allow it?' He seemed more amazed than Leyne herself. 'Don't you think, as her maybe father, that I have a right—?'

Her insides gave a panicky turnover. 'You have no rights whatsoever here!' Leyne snapped sharply. She wanted him to acknowledge that he was Pip's father, but heaven forbid he should claim parental rights over her!

Jack Dangerfield did not look in the least perturbed. 'Forgive me, Miss Rowberry,' he said urbanely, 'but don't you think that I, blood tie proven, have more rights than a half-aunt?'

And Leyne was totally stumped. She had not looked at any of this from his angle. Or, if she had, she had assumed that he would not be interested in playing any part in her upbringing. 'I'm her guardian! I have it in writing—appointed by her mother.' She began to get tough.

'But not her *legal* guardian.' He was tougher. And got even more tough when he went on, 'And who do you think would have more sway in court— you, or me?'

'Court! You'd take me to court?' Utterly dismayed at what she had started, with visions of Max returning home to find her daughter a ward of the court or something, Leyne gasped. 'You can't afford the publicity!' she attempted croakily.

'For anything to do with mine, I wouldn't care.' He shrugged. 'And, forgive me,' he asked, without sounding in the least apologetic, 'but can you afford it financially?'

'That's a low blow!' Leyne flared, hating this man opposite her suddenly.

Her accusation did not even dent him. She guessed he probably lived in a world where he sometimes had to play tough. 'So—I get to take her to tea?'

'Pip goes nowhere without me!' Leyne informed adamantly.

He smiled, and she just did not believe in his smile any more. 'If you're good,' he said nicely, 'you get to come too.'

Leyne sent him a furious look. 'It's not on!' she hissed between clenched teeth.

'Why isn't it?' he asked reasonably—and she hated him.

'For one thing, what do I tell Pip? How do I explain you to her?'

'Tell her I'm your boyfriend.'

Leyne tossed him a speaking look. 'I have a boyfriend. And,' she hurried on when it seemed he was about to interrupt, 'I shouldn't like Pip to get the idea that it's all right to run several boyfriends at one and the same time.'

'Ah!' Jack murmured softly. 'A little moralist.' Leyne wanted to thump him. Doubly so when, without the merest regret, he appeared to have the answer and said silkily, 'Oh, dear—it looks as though poor Keith has just been dumped.'

To her mind, Jack Dangerfield's solution did not dignify an answer. But for politeness' sake—though she was suddenly confused as to why she was bothering to be polite to the monster—Leyne made herself finish the rest of the meal. She was glad to be in the car and on her way back home again.

On the drive at her home she would quite happily have gone indoors without saying another word. But, as if fully aware of how she felt, Jack stopped her in her tracks by saying, 'Talking of money…' And as Leyne turned to stare at him in her surprise, he switched on the car's interior light and turned to face her.

'Money?' she asked, looking into those green eyes she knew so well. The only time that money had been mentioned that evening had been when he had suggested that she would not be able to meet him in court financially.

'I'd prefer to not discuss it tomorrow in front of Philippa,' he looked straight back at her to amicably confide, 'but are you sure you're all right with regard to getting her everything she needs?'

This man constantly took the wind from her sails! He had just done it again. 'You appear to have woken up to your responsibilities with a vengeance!' she retorted waspishly. And, before he could blind her with the science of some other unwanted comment, 'We want nothing from you—none of us!' she added hotly.

'Not even my name?' he quietly let fall.

He had jolted her again! She stared at him in horror—in truth she had no idea if her niece would want to take her father's name. Leyne drew a shaky breath, and guessed that her consternation over that issue must have shown in her expression because, ever a man with surprises, he surprised her again—by apologising.

'I'm sorry,' he said, and this time looked as

though he meant it. 'I know that for yourself you want nothing. We can discuss any possible name-change once we have clarified other matters.'

Other matters! *Name-change!* Heavens above, this was something she had not for a moment considered when she had written to him. The name Nicholson had been good enough for Pip so far; Max would have a fit!

Leyne opened her mouth, ready to tell him he could think again if he had any idea of giving Pip the Dangerfield title while still being unwilling to accept that he was her father. She closed it again. While lamenting—oh, what, what, *what* had she begun?—Leyne at that moment saw that any such decision was not hers to make.

There seemed nothing more to be said. 'Goodnight!' she offered grimly, and got out of the car, but only to find that he was at the front door with her.

'I'll see you tomorrow,' he said as she fumbled in her bag for her door key. 'Round about three,' he added, taking the key she'd found from her and inserting it into the lock. She stared at him as he opened the door, pushed it inwards, snicked on the hall light and handed her back the key. 'Goodnight, Leyne,' he bade her and, to her complete astonishment, he bent his head and kissed her cheek.

Blindly she walked forward, her mouth open in her startlement. She closed the door behind her. Over the racing of her heart she heard his car start up.

He had driven away down the drive but her heart was still thundering. Why? Leyne came away from the door, wondering why she should suddenly feel so, so—all over the place. Then decided it would be a wonder if she didn't. All in one and the same breath he had accepted, without *her* actually accepting, that he would take them out to tea tomorrow. And at the same time he had thrown in that other dimension of Pip possibly wanting to take her rightful name.

That was all that had thrown her, Leyne realised, and it had absolutely nothing to do with the fact that he had so astonishingly kissed her!

Pfff! she scorned. She had been kissed many times before, and more passionately, so she just knew that Jack Dangerfield kissing her on the cheek had nothing to do with it.

Good grief, the idea that his light kiss should have set her heart hammering so was just too ridiculous for words!

CHAPTER FOUR

BY MORNING Leyne had fully recovered her equilibrium and was quite clearly able to see that the only reason she had been in any way disquieted the previous evening was because of the staggering bombshell Jack Dangerfield had tossed her way with regard to the possibility of Pip wanting to take his name. It had nothing whatsoever to do with what, after all, had been merely some throwaway kiss, and everything, Leyne had to face, to do with the hornets' nest she had disturbed when trying to do what, in her guardianship, was right for her niece.

The house was quiet without Pip. Leyne wanted her home. She wanted her home safe with her. Though first she had to come up with something near to the truth to explain to Pip why this man she had once briefly met was taking them both out to tea.

When the phone rang, Leyne hastened to answer it. While she always enjoyed talking to her mother,

her spirits fell that it was not Max. 'Where's Pip?' Catherine Webb enquired of her granddaughter.

'She's on a sleepover at Alice's,' Leyne explained. 'She'll be in any time now.'

'Any news?' Catherine asked, realising Leyne would be able to speak freely. 'Has Mr Dangerfield been in touch?'

'He has,' Leyne was able to tell her. 'He now has the result of the DNA test. But apparently, while there is enough evidence to show that there's a blood link, it's not enough to prove that he is Pip's father.'

'He's denying that he is? Even with that evidence! I thought, from the little Maxine told me, that he was a more honourable man than that.'

'Well…' Leyne spotted Dianne's car coming up the drive. 'Subject normal,' she warned. 'Pip's just arriving.'

'What I really rang to tell you is that Roland has decided we need a pick-me-up after his "flu". He's arranged for his brother to have Suzie, and has booked a flight to the Canaries. By the sound of it the weather is much warmer there. We're off next Tuesday.'

'It will do you both good,' Leyne stated, the weather in England being particularly cold and miserable just then. 'How long will you be away?' she asked, returning Dianne's wave through the sitting room window.

'Could be weeks. Roland was talking in terms of looking at a villa and staying most of the winter there.'

'I shall miss you not being at the other end of a phone,' Leyne said, and knew that she would.

'They have phones in the Canaries, I believe,' her mother said dryly, and they both laughed.

'Here's Pip,' Leyne announced as Pip came into the sitting room, looking for her. 'Nanna,' Leyne explained, passing the phone over to her niece while feeling a tug at her heartstrings when Pip tried to hide her instant hope that it was Max on the line.

Leyne left Pip talking to her grandmother and went into the kitchen, still trying to think up some good reason to explain why Jack Dangerfield was calling to take them out to tea.

'Mrs Gardner said to forgive her for not coming in,' Pip said in a rush when she came to the kitchen. 'She has to be somewhere else. Alice thinks she's got a boyfriend—Mrs Gardner, not Alice,' Pip tacked on with a laugh.

'Have a good time?'

'Great!' Pip responded. And, recalling her aunt had arranged to dine with Keith Collins the previous evening, 'Where did Keith take you?'

'Actually,' Leyne began, 'I—um—didn't go out with Keith.'

'Crikey! Have you fallen out?'

Keith hadn't been thrilled, Leyne recalled, to put it mildly. 'Sort of,' she replied, which was probably not too much of a lie. 'Er—as a matter of fact, I had dinner with Jack Dangerfield.' And, while Pip's eyes went wide, 'Um—he wants to take you and me out to tea this afternoon.'

'Wow!' Pip exclaimed. And, like the dear child she was, 'He doesn't have to take me along too,' she said quickly.

'He doesn't?' Leyne had to smile. She knew perfectly well that it was only because of Pip that the outing had been proposed. Since Jack Dangerfield plainly was not the 'going out to Sunday afternoon tea' type, if Pip did not go, none of them would go.

'He doesn't want me tagging along!' Pip answered. 'It's you he's interested in, not me.'

Oh, sweetheart. Leyne wanted to hug her close and tell her everything. But she was not yet twelve, at a tender age, and Leyne could not bear to hurt her should she yield and tell her that, although he was without doubt her father, he was disowning that fact, disowning her.

'We're two musketeers,' Leyne said teasingly. 'Where I go, you go.'

'Love me, love my niece, eh?' Pip's lively sense of humour picked up.

Leyne laughed, and admitted, when a couple of hours later she and Pip ate a light lunch, that she did feel cheered. She guessed it was a combination of having Pip safe home and the fact that with the afternoon outing to look forward to Pip was not giving her any of those long, silently questioning looks.

When Jack Dangerfield's car pulled onto the

drive a minute or so before three, Leyne was ready. She opened the door to him, and for a crazy moment her heart picked up a ridiculous beat. 'Hello, Leyne Rowberry,' he greeted her, a charming upward curve on that rather wonderful mouth that had last night kissed her cheek.

Wonderful! For heaven's sake! 'Come in,' she invited, aware of his light gaze flicking over her trim shape in her sage-coloured trouser suit. 'Pip won't be a moment.'

Leyne led the way into the sitting room and was amazed to find she was feeling all at sixes and sevens suddenly. 'Um…' she began, searching a little desperately for a topic of conversation. 'Er— Pip won't be…' She did not have to finish. Foot- steps hurrying down the stairs told them that Pip was about to join them.

'Saved by the bell,' Jack murmured, and Leyne began to hate that about him that he apparently knew so much about women, that he knew exactly how awkward she was feeling.

'I'm not late?' Pip asked, rushing in.

'Not at all,' Jack assured her, and Leyne just knew he had spotted—as she just had—that Pip, growing all the time, had shot up again since she had last worn her best trousers. They were a good two inches too short for her.

'You've grown out of those,' Leyne commented lightly. Max was a dainty five feet three—and already Pip was taller than her mother. Clearly the Dangerfields were a lofty breed.

'Shall I go and change?' Pip asked hesitantly.

'Wouldn't hear of it,' Jack said immediately, and confided, 'Those are the prettiest pair of ankles I've seen all day.'

Pip giggled, and then the phone rang. 'Ooh, I said I'd ring Alice—and I forgot!' she exclaimed, hurrying over to the phone. 'Sorry, Al,' she apologised, listened, and then said, 'Sorry,' again, adding, 'I can't. I'm going out to tea with Leyne and her new boyfriend.'

Oh, grief! Leyne felt herself colour up and just would not look at Jack, and was glad that for once Pip kept her conversation with her friend short.

Jack, with Pip insisting that her aunt sit up front with her 'boyfriend', drove them to a small country hotel and kept up a pleasant conversation with them both. Leyne rather formed an impression that he would be comfortable in any set of surroundings, be it in high-powered talks with captains of industry or, as now, as host taking a schoolgirl and her aunt out to tea.

Although in this case, Leyne mused sourly, the schoolgirl in question was his daughter. And while he, having invited Pip to call him Jack when she had called him Mr Dangerfield a few times, might not be ready to admit it yet, Leyne just knew it was so.

And a few minutes later, when both Pip and

their host broke into grins as they reached for the sole éclair at the same time, any stray strand of doubt vanished completely. They even grinned in identical fashion. Green eyes mirth-filled, heads slightly back, and an identical small cough of laughter.

'Cake?' Jack offered the cakestand to Leyne a moment later.

'We didn't have very much lunch,' Pip chipped in, leaving Leyne short of her excuse that she had just eaten a sandwich and was still full up from lunch, while at the same time causing her to want to make excuses because by now Jack Dangerfield would think she was starving his daughter. But relief was at hand when Pip went on to explain, 'Leyne thought it would be bad manners to accept your invitation to tea and then not eat anything because of our usual Sunday roast and pud.'

Which, of course, brought his eyes to Leyne. 'You are one heck of a lady,' he observed quietly.

Oh, heavens, there went that bumpity heart thing again. 'In that case I'll claim that last éclair,' she said. And while the other two sat and gaped at her, she quickly snaffled it.

It was good, the matching looks of amusement that followed a split second later. And Leyne grinned too. She realised on the homeward drive that, not having wanted to come on this little jaunt, and certainly having been against him taking Pip out to tea, she had very much enjoyed the time with him. As for Pip, she seemed to be highly animated.

However, enough was enough for one day. 'Thank you for a lovely afternoon,' Leyne thanked him pleasantly when, on the drive of her home, he got out of the car too.

'Are you coming in?' Pip invited him.

'I've—er—one or two jobs to do,' Leyne butted in quickly.

'Leyne always checks on Sunday that everything's ready for me for school on Monday and work for her,' Pip explained.

'I thought you worked from home sometimes?' Jack turned to Leyne to query.

'I do, but—'

'My mum says that Paget and Company are very lucky to have Leyne,' Pip, at her most talkative, chipped in.

'I'm sure your mum is right,' Jack responded courteously—and Leyne had had enough.

'We'll see you, Jack.' She terminated the conversation affably, reaching out to give Pip a reminding prod.

'Thank you very much for my tea,' Pip responded on cue.

'The pleasure was all mine,' he said, and took a step back.

'Bye, Jack,' Leyne bade him politely.

'Bye, Jack,' Pip echoed with a beam of a smile,

and Leyne ushered her indoors. She felt sure Jack would not have come in anyway. It was now late afternoon, merging into early evening—he would have other fish to fry.

No sooner were she and Pip indoors than Pip was on the phone to her friend Alice, giving her a blow-by-blow account of her afternoon. 'He's great!' Leyne heard her enthuse, 'great' being her word of the moment. 'Much better than that cruddy Keith Leyne used to go out with!'

Cruddy Keith ignored her at work the next day, and on Tuesday too. But on Wednesday, perhaps piqued that she appeared to be able to live quite cheerfully without his approval, he, to her surprise, stopped by her desk.

'I need to be more understanding, don't I?' he asked, a little-boy-lost look playing around his not very substantial mouth—she had never noticed his mean mouth before.

'I—um…' Leyne brought herself quickly together. 'You know the situation,' she reminded him.

'Shall we have another try?'

Suddenly she was not at all bothered. But against that she *had* rather let him down a time or two. 'I've the offer of a sitter for Friday,' she volunteered. Dianne Gardner had confided that she was dating an airline pilot. The relationship was in its early stages, and, because he was not often free at the weekends he wanted to take her out tomorrow.

Dianne had asked if Alice could possibly sleep at their place on Thursday night. In return Dianne had offered to have Pip any time over the weekend to suit. Leyne would have agreed to have Alice stay anyway. Dianne had been through a very unpleasant divorce—it was time that something nice happened for her.

Keith went on his way, saying he would book a table at a new Indian restaurant he had heard of, and Leyne got down to some work.

At home that night she had a phone call from Brazil. It was not from her sister, however, but from a man calling himself Urbano, with a surname she just did not catch. 'Senhor Turnbull say to tell you how are you?' he asked, in such a thickly accented voice that Leyne had to concentrate hard to know what he was saying.

'Maxine, my sister, she is not able to phone?' Leyne asked, realising as she asked the question that Max and Ben Turnbull must still be photographing in some very out-of-the-way place—or why else get someone else to telephone? 'Um…' she wanted to ask him to ask Max to phone her at her first opportunity, but Leyne knew that Max would regard that as a priority anyway.

'The lady is worried for you,' Urbano stated, before Leyne could sort out what sort of message she should give him. 'I must ask for her daughter.'

'Worried?' Leyne queried, even as she asked realising that, while she knew not even the first smat-tering of Portuguese, Urbano was perhaps not using his English in quite the right context. Though she thought she knew what he was asking. 'We are both well,' she informed him, guessing he would be going back to wherever they had made camp—he had probably had to return to some replenishment point to pick up supplies.

'Her daughter?' Urbano asked.

'Her daughter is very well,' Leyne told him. 'Just a moment,' she added, and, aware of Pip hovering, 'You can speak to her yourself.' Leyne turned. 'Come and say hello to this gentleman. He's phoning on behalf of your mother,' she relayed, holding out the phone to Pip.

'Hello?' Pip said obediently. Pause, then, 'Yes, I am Philippa.' Another pause, then Pip looked at Leyne. 'I think he's asking me how I am.'

'Then tell him, sweetheart.'

'I am very well, thank you,' Pip said into the phone, and started to ask, 'Is—?' Then she turned to Leyne and handed back the phone. 'I think he's gone.'

Leyne listened. The line was dead. 'Well, wasn't that good?' she said with a smile. 'It would have been better to have spoken to your mum in person. But, since she must be out in the wilds somewhere, wasn't it lovely of her to ask Urbano to get in touch?'

'If she had rung you could have asked her about

my dad,' Pip commented, lest Leyne had forgotten all about it.

'Try and be patient a little longer, ' Leyne replied, feeling mean. But her first concern was to see to it that Pip did not get hurt. And hurt she would be if she knew that Jack Dangerfield was refusing to acknowledge her.

'You're still making enquiries?'

'Nothing—concrete. But as soon as I've got some good news to share, you'll be the first to know,' Leyne promised.

Anticipating she might be delayed by getting two young ladies up and ready for school on Friday—strictures to not sit up talking the whole night meeting with only limited success—Leyne decided to work from home.

Having delivered both girls to school, Leyne returned home to make order out of the mini chaos that was the kitchen, and to strip the bed Alice had used. By ten-thirty she was busy at her computer. She was still there, because of her late start working through her lunch hour, when someone rang the doorbell.

She had been too absorbed in what she was doing to have heard a car pull up on the drive, but as she left the small study and took a quick glance through the sitting room window, so she saw a car parked there that looked very familiar. Leyne went out into the hall musing that if she was not mistaken it was the same car that she and Pip had journeyed in last Sunday.

And all at once Leyne's heart started to hurry up its beat. Even as she told herself she was being crazy—why on earth would Jack Dangerfield pay her a call in the middle of the day?—she was reaching with a slightly shaking hand to unlatch the door.

It was him! Jack, green-eyed, raven-haired, Dangerfield, business-suited—and handsome enough to make the legs of any impressionable female turn to water.

Only she wasn't impressionable, and while he silently took in her slightly flushed face, gorgeous eyes and fantastic complexion, Leyne was certain she was not going to be the first to speak.

She was, of course. He had an uncanny knack of unnerving her, it seemed. It was a freezing cold day. 'Come in,' she found she was inviting, 'It's bitter out there.'

Without comment he stepped over the threshold. Leyne was in two minds to let him say what he had come to say where he stood in the hall. But courtesy won the day and she invited him into the sitting room.

'Not working today?' she asked, moving to put some space between them—this man seemed to be getting to her in a most peculiar way!

'I'm allowed a lunch break,' he answered, a mocking kind of light there in his eyes.

'I'm working through my lunch today,' she said

pointedly, and could have kicked herself when she found she was explaining, 'I had a late start.' She decided to take charge. 'How did you know I'd be here? I could have been working from the office.'

'You weren't. I rang.'

'You rang my office?' He didn't know where she worked! Correction. Yes, he did; Pip had told him. Leyne looked up at him, and when he made no reply, 'Why?' she demanded. And, rapidly growing all defensive about her niece, 'Why did you want to see me? What have you decided—?'

'There's no need to panic,' Jack cut her off smoothly. And, coming straight to the point, 'I have a property down at the south coast. I thought Pip might like to come with me for the weekend.'

'You—'

'Since we'll be away until Sunday, it suddenly occurred to me it would be more polite if I gave you a few hours' notice. Perhaps I shouldn't expect you to pack a few clothes at a moment's notice when I call after close of business today.'

Leyne stared at him, open-mouthed at his sauce. 'Pip's going nowhere with you,' she told him bluntly when she had her breath back.

'No?'

Leyne did not like that he did not appear at all worried. 'No,' she said firmly. And when he just stood there, not budging, and certainly not giving in, 'Why do you want to take her anyway?' she demanded.

'I think it's more than high time I got to know her,' he replied, unblinking.

Leyne gave him a frosty look as she strove hard to know what to do for the best—for Pip. Jack had just said that he wanted to get to know her. Was she being fair in denying Pip the right to know him?

'You're ready to admit that you're her father?' she challenged.

'No!' he stated forthrightly.

'Then she stays here.'

'I don't think so,' he replied, quite pleasantly. Leyne wanted to hit him.

'No!' she repeated, refusing to budge.

'Why not?' he queried, and she hated him that he managed to sound quite reasonable—which made *her* sound totally *un*reasonable!

'Because, apart from anything else, Pip would think it odd—her going off with you on her own when—'

'We won't be on our own,' he cut in charmingly.

'You're taking Gina?' Leyne could have bitten out her tongue, but too late now. Grief, she had actually sounded jealous! What rot!

'Gina?'

'You were pictured with her in a paper I saw when I wanted to find you,' Leyne had to explain.

His mouth quirked upwards at the corners. 'How did Gina get into this?' Leyne, this time, refused to

answer. 'I no longer see Gina,' he went on to en-
lighten her.

'Of course you don't!' Leyne retorted, wondering how long he kept a girlfriend before he told
her bye-bye.

'Nor would I take just any woman down to Sherbourne,' he added for her information, when she
was sure she didn't give a button which of his women-friends he took to his south coast property, or
how many. He was still not taking Pip. A moment
later, though, and she was staring at him wide-eyed
and completely dumbfounded when he casually
informed her, 'I'm taking you,'

'Me!' Leyne exclaimed. He could go and take a
running jump!

'But of course you,' he agreed, adding, and
making it sound as if he believed he was being
completely rational, 'I know nothing at all about
eleven-year-old girls—even if I *am* the father of one
in particular.'

Leyne stared at him. This was the closest he had
come to admitting that he was Pip's father. Yet,
somehow, while conceding that this was indeed
progress, Leyne sensed a threat behind that, 'even
if I *am* the father.'

'I…' she began, angry with him, and angry with
herself that because of him she had never felt so all
at sea, so not knowing what was the best for her niece.
'I—I've got a date tonight,' she exploded frustratedly.

'Keith doesn't appear to be having much luck,' Jack drawled, not moving an inch from his intention that they journey to the south coast later that day.

It was a truth, however, that all at once, startlingly, dawned on Leyne, that she would as much enjoy Jack Dangerfield's company as she would that of Keith Collins! 'He's—not going to like it,' she said, barely realising that she had just about agreed that she and Pip *would* go to this place Sherbourne that evening.

'He knows about Pip?' Jack demanded, his expression all at once stern.

'Of course he knows about her. I wouldn't dream of leaving her alone while I go out with—'

'Not that!' Jack cut her off. 'The fact that the child is asking about her father?'

'That's private!' Leyne erupted. 'He knows Pip is my sister's child, and that's all he needs to know,'

Jack Dangerfield was back to being mocking again. 'Not very close, are you?'

He had a knack, Leyne decided, of being deliberately irritating. One of these days... 'My closeness or not with Keith Collins is beside the point,' she flared hotly. 'This issue is much too sensitive to discuss with anyone but those directly concerned. For your—'

'You're lovely when you've got your dander up,' Jack butted in, a smile breaking so disarmingly across his features that she felt that fluttery feeling in her heart region again.

'Not only in a good light, then!' she retorted, while scorning that she felt in any way fluttery about the wretched man.

'You're beautiful in any light,' he stated, and seemed so sincere all of a sudden that Leyne, unexpectedly experiencing a breathless kind of feeling, abruptly turned away from him.

'I'll show you out,' she decided, feeling mean that, this being his lunch hour after all, she hadn't offered him so much as a cup of coffee.

'Until later,' he said by her side.

Leyne was glad to see him go, and once his car was away from the drive she sank down into a chair. This man Dangerfield was having a most peculiar effect on her.

Not that that was so surprising, she was able to rationalise a few minutes later. While Pip's well-being was still paramount, Leyne could not help but be anxious over what she had done, and about how Max would view all of this. What on earth she would have to say when she knew that she and Pip had spent the weekend with Pip's father, Leyne could not begin to guess.

And yet while on the one hand starting to regret that she had ever contacted Jack Dangerfield in the first place, Leyne knew deep down that, presented with the same set of circumstances again, in Pip's interests she would do exactly the same. And, on the up-side, it seemed to her that, from his 'if I *am* the father' remark, Jack was starting to accept that Pip *was* his.

Though why he had called in person when he had their home phone number, and had used it before, Leyne failed to see. Perhaps he'd thought he would be better able to persuade her to go with him to this place called Sherbourne by making a personal visit.

Much persuading had he had to do, she derided herself scornfully. She had folded almost without a fight. Peculiar wasn't the word for the effect he had on her—though what word she could substitute for it, Leyne just could not think.

But this wasn't getting any work done. She sprang up from her chair—and then realised she had a couple of phone calls to make.

Her call to Dianne to explain that she would not now need her to have Pip because they would be away for the weekend went with very little problem—other than that Dianne seemed to know all about her new boyfriend Jack from her daughter Alice.

'Have a lovely time,' Dianne bade her.

Leyne's phone call to Keith Collins did not end nearly so harmoniously. 'You can't make tonight!' he exclaimed, scandalised. 'You're not serious?'

'I'm sorry, Keith,' she apologised guiltily, knowing she was in the wrong, but between a rock and a hard place. Jack Dangerfield wanted to get to know his daughter, and, from where Leyne was viewing it, how could she stop him? Or, for that matter, who was she to stop him?

'It's that kid again, isn't it?' Keith snapped nastily.

He could not have said anything more guaranteed to have that shroud of guilt melt from her. 'That kid', as he called her in such derogatory tones, was her lovely, sweet, never-done-any-harm-to-anyone Pip—her dear sister's child.

'Goodbye, Keith,' Leyne said, and put down the phone. *Now* to get on with some work.

Dianne picked up both girls from school and, as discussed with Leyne, and contrary to their usual arrangement, dropped Pip off. She had not, Leyne discovered, said anything to Pip about their telephone conversation. And, Leyne, still wary that Pip might end up being hurt if Jack would not admit parenthood, was left with no option but to carry on the myth that he was her boyfriend when she asked, 'How do you fancy a weekend at the south coast with Jack and me?'

'Which weekend?' Pip asked, her face alight.

'This weekend.'

'Like—tomorrow?' Pip questioned, and, with a grin, 'Wow, he's keen! Dinner tonight, south coast tomorrow.'

Guiltily Leyne realised she could not have said who her dinner date had been with that night. And Pip—naturally enough, Leyne supposed—had assumed she had been going out with Jack Dangerfield. 'Actually, Jack's calling for us tonight when he finishes work.'

'Great!' Pip exclaimed. 'Can I ring and tell Alice? She'll have to know I'm not going swimming tomorrow, anyway.'

Because of the interruptions to her day, not to mention a break while she packed an overnight bag for Pip and one for herself, Leyne was filling in time in the study while waiting for Jack to call.

She heard the doorbell, though, when it rang. 'I'll go!' Pip called, which gave Leyne the few minutes she needed at her computer to save and print the material she was working on.

She was in the middle of transferring matter from her desk into her briefcase, ready to take to her place of work on Monday, when, glancing to the open study door, she saw Jack and Pip standing there—Jack silently eyeing her.

'I won't keep you waiting more than a few minutes,' she said, feeling her cheeks warm for no reason.

'Take as much time as you need,' Jack answered quietly, his glance steady on her.

'Jack said to take our Wellingtons. Shall I go and get them?' Pip piped up.

'Good idea,' Leyne replied smilingly.

'She seems excited,' Jack observed as Pip scampered off.

Leyne closed her briefcase and looked at him. 'We do as much as we can.'

'I wasn't criticising,' he said, coming close. And, looking down into her lovely blue eyes, 'Believe me, Leyne, I think you do marvellously.'

She felt choked all at once. 'This—study isn't big enough for two,' she muttered huskily, and edged round him.

Pip helped Jack stow their belongings in the boot of his car while Leyne locked up the house. But when Leyne went to join her in the back seat of his car, 'Sit up front with Jack,' Pip suggested thoughtfully.

'I...'

'You've gone shy on me,' Jack taunted, opening the front passenger door for her.

It would not have been quite the thing to thump him in front of her niece. Without a word Leyne got into the front.

Pip had always been, for the most part, a fairly serious child. While there were times when she would forget her more sober side and go off into a fit of giggles if something amused her, the more solemn, serious side generally prevailed.

But that car ride to Jack's south coast property was something of a revelation to Leyne. Jack had stated that he wanted to get to know his blood relative, and, presumably to that end, soon struck up a harmonious conversation with Pip. The revelation was, however, the way in which the eleven-year-old responded.

Indeed, for such a reserved child, it seemed to

Leyne at one stage that Pip was asking all the questions.

'Leyne says we're going to somewhere called Sherbourne,' she opened up at one stage.

'That's the name of the house,' Jack enlightened her. 'It's on the edge of a village called Dalingbury.'

'Is it near the sea?'

'The sea's about ten minutes away by car. But it will be too cold to go for a swim at this time of year.'

'I don't mind missing my swim tomorrow,' Pip told him cheerfully. And, later on, when she must have noticed they had been driving for quite some while, 'Do you live at Sherbourne during the week? It seems a long way to come every day.'

Leyne wondered if she should perhaps mention that Jack might quite like silence to concentrate on his driving, but he and Pip seemed to have such a natural consanguinity with each other that Leyne hesitated to butt in. In any event, he answered quite cheerfully enough that he had an apartment in London where he stayed most nights of the week. And Leyne could not help but wonder if, while she and Max did everything they could to make Pip feel she was missing out on nothing, something *had* been missing, that they could not give her: a father figure in her life!

Such thoughts kept Leyne quiet for long stretches of time, so that she added very little to the conversation. On balance, she began to consider that she had done the right thing in agreeing to allow Pip this visit to Sherbourne. Though, from memory, she didn't think that when Jack Dangerfield had declared he would like to take Pip to his south coast property this weekend he had given her aunt very much choice in the matter.

But Pip, having used up her questions for a while, was, as Jack had observed, excited, and her enquiring mind would not be still for too long. 'Do you have anyone else living with you at Sherbourne?' She asked a question Leyne had not thought of.

'Just me,' he answered lightly.

'I'll help you make up our beds,' Pip volunteered happily.

'Already done,' Jack informed her. 'I've a very nice lady, Mrs Ford—she lives in the village—who will have made everything ready for us. Now, tell me, how are you getting on at school?'

'This is my first term at this new school. It's great,' Pip replied, and regaled him sunnily with her various exploits and the various merits of her teachers. She was too sweet a child to mention any demerits there might be.

By the time they reached the village of Dalingbury, the back and forward conversation between Pip and Jack had revealed that they shared a love of books, Pip being an avid reader, and, as far as Leyne could see, they had an identical sense of humour, in that what set Pip into laughter mode also made Jack smile.

Sherbourne, when they pulled round in front of it, was an old period style building. And, on going inside, the house appeared to have been entirely re-furbished. 'We'll just take your bags up to your rooms, then we'll see about supper,' Jack suggested.

Pip was highly delighted with her room, which had its own bathroom. They left her unpacking her weekend bag, and Jack showed Leyne a similar but larger room next door.

'Sing out if you need anything,' he said, and, excusing himself, 'I'll go and see if I can follow Mrs Ford's instructions with the microwave.'

Left to herself, Leyne took in her lovely room. It was a very feminine room for such a bachelor house-hold, with the palest of pink walls, cream carpet and cream-coloured heavy winter curtains. She too had an adjoining bathroom, Leyne saw. She had just unzipped her toilet bag when Pip came to find her.

'Wow!' she exclaimed. 'I thought my room was lovely, but...' She looked around. 'Wow!' she said again.

'We'll eat soon. Have you washed your hands?'

They found Jack downstairs in the kitchen. 'Anything I can do?' Pip took the words out of Leyne's mouth, and Leyne, looking on at father and daughter, had to smile.

Trust Jack Dangerfield to look across at just that moment, his eyes on her smiling eyes, his glance straying down to her beautiful upturned mouth.

Leyne looked from him to Pip, who was contentedly surveying a 'pinging' microwave. 'I think this weekend will do us all good,' broke from Leyne before she had a chance to stop it.

Her eyes went to Jack again. 'That's very generous of you to say so,' he remarked quietly. And Leyne guessed he must be thinking of her initial opposition to coming here to his south coast home.

Supper was a very pleasant mealtime, with Leyne being proud of Pip and her natural good manners. Leyne had to admit too that she warmed to Jack for his pleasant way with Pip.

Woman power prevailed, however, when at the end of the meal she and Pip overruled his declaration that they were guests and that *he* would clear away and attend to their used dishes on his own.

'If you insist,' he gave in, with a grin to Pip— which made it fairly obvious that he'd had no intention of doing the dishes on his own anyway.

Leyne tossed him an 'I've seen through you' look, accompanied by the light comment, 'That's why you're in management.'

His grin encompassed her too. But, in any event, while they all set to and tidied up the dining room and kitchen, it appeared he had an automatic dishwasher.

Talk thereafter got around to books, with Jack allowing them *carte blanche* to raid his library. 'We've brought books with us,' Leyne answered.

'Both Pip and I like to read for a short while before going to sleep.'

'That's something else we have in common,' he commented.

'Shall I go up now?' Pip asked.

'I'll come with you,' Leyne answered.

'Goodnight, Jack,' Pip said, and seemed shy all at once, on her way from the room.

'Goodnight, poppet,' he said gently. But when Leyne went to follow her, Jack caught a hold of her arm, detaining her. 'Look,' he said as Leyne glanced up at him, 'I know your first concern is Pip, and count on it I'm with you on that.'

'You are?'

'Trust me,' he said.

All of a sudden Leyne wanted to be able to trust him. To some degree she supposed she must trust him, or she would have taken steps somehow to prevent their coming here with him tonight.

'I want to,' she confessed, feeling all breathless in the scrutiny of his steady green-eyed gaze. 'But…'

'I promise she'll be all right,' he said quietly. 'Pip is one most delightful, quiet-thinking, sparkling youngster.' He smiled into Leyne's eyes and added winningly, 'Confidentially, and just between you and me, I'd be proud to claim her as one of my kin.'

His smile, his hold on her arm, was making her spine go weak. But from somewhere Leyne found some stiffening. This was not about her; it was about Pip. 'But not proud enough to claim her as your daughter?' she challenged coldly.

His lips firmed and he abruptly let go her arm. Hostile blue eyes stared into instantly aloof green eyes. There seemed nothing more to be said. Leyne, with sadness in her heart, walked from him, and from the room.

CHAPTER FIVE

LEYNE was awake early the following morning, but, because she was a guest in someone else's house she thought, just in case she woke everyone else, to delay taking her shower.

She had no idea what plans, if any, Jack might have for the day, but she and Pip were quite capable of amusing themselves if he was going to be busy elsewhere. Snicking on her bedside light, she saw it had only just gone six.

Reaching for her book, she thought to read for a while. Yet, strangely, unless her book of the moment was very dire she was usually able to absorb herself in what she was reading, that morning though her thoughts kept straying to Jack Dangerfield, their host.

Pip could sometimes be a little diffident with new people, but, given her moment of shyness last night, Leyne was a little amazed at how confident Pip was with him. Was that blood calling to blood?

Leyne recalled the cold way she herself had parted from him. And she felt a spurt of annoyance with him again that, when it was so obvious that he was Pip's father, he was still refusing to acknowledge that fact.

Well, tough, Leyne bridled, starting to get angry. The very next time Pip asked that question, or even looked at her asking that question, she was going to tell her.

But as that thought was born, so Leyne's flare of anger fizzled out. How could she tell her—only to have her hurt when Jack denied it? Besides that, would Max want her to?

Leyne was in the middle of being torn all ways when a whisper of sound over by the door drew her eyes in that direction. A pyjama clad Pip stood there, book in hand. Softly she tiptoed in and quietly closed the door. 'I thought you'd be reading,' she whispered, coming over to the bed. 'Room for a little one?'

Pip had plainly had enough sleep and, an early riser too, was also anxious not to disturb their host. Leyne wondered if, having awakened in a strange room, she had felt just a touch insecure and had come looking for her. 'Climb in,' Leyne invited lightly, pulling back the covers.

They read for a half-hour, then Leyne thought she heard the sound of Jack moving around. She left Pip reading and went and had her shower.

'Trousers today, do you think?' Pip enquired, getting ready to return to her own room.

'Yes, I think so. I don't know what plans Jack might have, but you and I can go for a walk if he's busy.'

It was just before eight when together they went down the stairs. 'Good morning, Leyne, Pip.' Jack, in the kitchen before them, greeted them, last night's small chill completely put away. 'Sleep well?'

'It's a lovely bed,' Pip replied—which left Leyne wanting to explain that she had as good and as lovely a bed at home.

I'm being defensive, she scolded a second later. Children are like that. 'Anything we can do?' she volunteered.

'Just tell me what you'd like for breakfast. Bacon, egg…' he began.

Only to learn from Pip, 'We usually just have cereal and fruit at home.'

'I'll cook bacon and egg for you, if you like,' Leyne offered their host.

He declined, and joined them for cereal and fruit, with toast thrown in. During which he asked Pip, 'What would you like to do today?'

'Leyne thought you might be busy.'

He transferred his gaze to Leyne, his eyes resting on her. 'I'm taking the weekend off,' he said, and set Leyne's pulses racing when, his eyes still on her, he seemed to like what he saw.

'We thought we might go for a walk.' She

overcame the idiotic notion that just his look could make her pulses race.

'That's where your Wellies will come in handy,' he answered, looking back to Pip. 'Fancy a walk on the beach?'

'Could we?' she asked excitedly.

An hour later, with jeans tucked into Wellington boots, and car parking easier at that time of year, the three of them were walking on wet sand. The weather was cold, the wind blustery, and for no reason she could think of, as the three of them strode across the deserted beach, Leyne felt she had never been happier.

Several times Pip ran on in front. 'Keith broken-hearted?' Jack asked Leyne on one such occasion.

She felt like laughing. 'You care?' she asked lightly.

'Dump him,' he instructed. 'He's not the man for you,' he assured her—and she just could not hold that laugh in.

'You know nothing about him!' she protested, her face turned up to Jack, her eyes laughter filled.

He stopped dead. Leyne stopped with him, a question in her look. 'Isn't it odd?' he said, almost in disbelief himself. 'Here you are, your hair all tousled and blown back any old how from your face, wind-tears on your cheeks, and yet—I think you are the most beautiful woman I've ever seen.'

Her heart thumped. She stared at him speechlessly and sought to find words. He raised a hand to her cheek and gently brushed those wind-tears away. Her breath caught; she thought he was about to kiss her. He looked as though to kiss her was his natural instinct. And just then, speechlessly silent as they stared into each other's eyes, there seemed to be no one else in the world except just—the two of them.

The sound of a dog furiously barking shattered the moment. Leyne swallowed, came to—and, with a quick check ahead to see that Pip was safe, was still struggling to find words.

'You should get out more,' was the best she could manage—Jack gave a small laugh, and they walked on.

Pip—having found a friend in a lady who had appeared and who was walking a large wet dog—was having the time of her life throwing a stick for it. The lady walked by with returned 'Good mornings' and Pip ran to them, her face alight. By the look of it, Leyne mused, her heartbeats still not quite settled down, she was not the only one to be in the happiest frame of mind.

'Shall we go and find somewhere for a coffee?' Jack asked about five minutes later, and as they turned about his glance went down to Pip. 'Or whatever it is that young ladies drink.'

'Great!' Already Pip was scampering off in front. Her friend with the dog called Mabel was too far in front by that time, though, for her to be able to throw any more sticks.

Jack was silent with his own thoughts as they retraced their steps across the sand. And Leyne, owning to still feeling shaken by his declaration that—oddly—it seemed she appeared to him to be the most beautiful woman he had ever seen, had nothing she wanted to say either.

They were almost at the spot where they had first stepped onto the beach when Pip, having run on ahead and now waiting for them, began to cough. 'Excuse me,' Leyne muttered, and was off.

She reached Pip in no time flat, and, outwardly calm, bent to check her. As she straightened she was aware that Jack had not wasted any time either, and was right there with them.

It was a comfort to know that he was there, but her priority then was her niece. Stretching out a hand, she felt Pip's forehead. She was boiling. 'See what stick-throwing for dogs you haven't been introduced to will get you,' she teased, at the same time noting Pip's distressed and breathless condition. Leyne plunged her hand into Pip's overcoat pocket and found the inhaler she should never be without. 'Sit down here for a minute,' she instructed, outwardly untroubled, her voice matter-of-fact. And, when her niece was seated on an adjacent boulder, 'Take a puff,' she said, shaking the inhaler and handing it to her. And, a minute or so later, 'And another one,' she instructed.

'Anything I can do?' Jack asked quietly in her ear.

'She'll be all right in a minute or two,' Leyne answered, buttoning Pip's coat up to the neck. 'But I'd like her to rest for a short while.'

'We'll go home,' he decided. 'Just say when, and I'll take her back to the car.'

By 'I'll take her back to the car' he meant carry her there, she realised when, Pip looking less breathless and less stressed, Leyne suggested they get out of the wind.

'I can walk,' Pip protested with a smile when Jack bent and picked her up.

'This is your penalty for doing me out of my coffee,' he told her severely, and she giggled.

This time on the drive to Sherbourne Leyne sat in the back with her. And at the house, when Jack would have carried Pip up to bed, Leyne stopped him. 'She'll be all right on the sofa, if that's all right,' she stated. And, thinking to give him something to do, since he might not have witnessed someone in an asthma attack before, 'Any good at making coffee?' She smiled—and Jack went kitchenwards.

Leyne got Pip out of her coat and Wellingtons and felt her head again. Only then, when Pip's forehead felt much less hot than it had, did she let go of some of her tension.

'I'll just pop and get you a drink,' she told Pip. Removing her own Wellingtons, she picked up the two pairs and took them with her as she hastened to the kitchen. 'I hope you don't mind Pip recovering in the drawing room,' she said to Jack, leaving the Wellingtons by the rear door. 'But I want her in normal surroundings and where I can see her.'

Just then Pip started to cough again, and Leyne, pausing only to pour a glass of water, did not wait for anything else.

It always amazed her that within a half-hour Pip was back to normal. But Leyne was in no hurry to go anywhere, and confided in Jack that she would be quite happy for Pip to stay indoors with her book.

Jack seemed relieved too that Pip's asthma attack was so soon over. And smiled kindly at her when she apologised and asked him, 'Am I being a nuisance?'

'Think nothing of it,' he answered, but added severely, 'Only don't grow any heavier!'

Since, though tall for her age, Pip was as slender as a wand, she knew he was jokingly referring to having carried her, and she laughed, clearly liking her aunt's 'boyfriend'.

'Shall we have a snack lunch and go out for an early dinner?' he asked.

Pip's excursions into dinner out totalled nil. She beamed at him, undeniably a very happy child.

She went with Leyne to see what help they could be with making lunch. But there was little to do, Mrs Ford having purchased prepared salads.

After a light meal Jack excused himself. Leyne heard him drive away, and supposed that being stuck indoors with two females was not quite what he had bargained for.

She was on the point of wondering if she should suggest they should go back home when, to her surprise, Jack returned. He had only popped out to find a couple of jigsaw puzzles, it transpired. And, to further surprise her, he seemed content to spend the whole afternoon working on them.

They had a short break for an afternoon cup of tea, but Jack, appearing to be enjoying his labours, seemed as eager as Pip to return to jigsaw-making.

When at around six Leyne and Pip went upstairs to freshen up and change, Leyne had to admit that when Jack had said that he wanted to get to know Pip, he had meant it.

Not that he had spent the whole afternoon asking questions, but they were communicating parts of themselves with every word they said. With every action too, as when Pip had forgotten her own section of the puzzle and gone to help him with his corner when he was sure that there was a piece missing. And Jack, likewise, had helped Pip to find an edge piece that had seemed to be absent. They'd given a joint whoop of pleasure when the last piece was pressed in. Clearly they enjoyed each other's company—as Leyne enjoyed theirs.

Leyne, with affection in her heart for them both, found as she took a quick shower that she was smiling. Affection! For him! She suddenly caught herself up short. Oh, for goodness' sake. Without question Pip held a huge chunk of her heart. But Jack Dangerfield?

Jack had booked a table at a very nice restaurant and was the perfect host all through dinner, treating Pip like a grown-up even to the extent of asking Leyne if she might, on this very celebratory occasion, be allowed a small glass of wine.

Leyne was instinctively ready to say no, but when she saw that the wine he was pouring for Pip was very much watered down, she could not argue.

'What are we celebrating?' Pip wanted to know.

'It's not every day that I find myself in the company of two of the best-looking women in the room,' he answered.

Pip blushed, and Leyne knew then that Jack had one very devoted fan. She hoped with all she had that he would treat her niece's sensitivities carefully. Though had to own that, so far, she had nothing to complain over on the score.

'That was the best meal I ever tasted,' Pip sighed as they left the restaurant.

Leyne smiled at her. How could she be defensive about the many, many meals *she* had cooked for her? The meal had truly been excellent, but Pip, she knew, was referring to the whole lovely experience of her first dinner out.

It was still early when they got back to Sherbourne. 'Tired, poppet?' Jack asked when, as they entered the house, she yawned.

'Leyne and I were awake ages early this morning,' she answered. 'We were reading in bed,' she added, in case he thought that getting downstairs for eight o'clock was not excessively early.

'Want to go to bed now?'

'Is that all right, Leyne?'

'Perfectly,' Leyne agreed, but suddenly realised that if Pip went up to bed she would be left downstairs alone with Jack. 'I think I'll come up too,' she said lightly.

'You wouldn't care for a nightcap?' Jack enquired.

For a moment Leyne had the craziest notion that he was a touch disappointed that she intended to leave. Get real, jolted the voice of reason. He was used to much more sophisticated company. That hint of regret was all part of his charm and nothing more.

'Oh, no thanks,' she answered with a smile. 'Goodnight. Oh, and thank you for a lovely day—and evening.'

Leyne could not remember the last time she had been in bed for half past nine. Which was a pity, because it seemed to take her hours and hours to get to sleep.

But eventually she did drift off—and slept soundly. In fact she was still sound away when the whisper of her bedroom door opening penetrated.

She supposed that like all mothers—in her case proxy mother—she slept with an ear open for her offspring.

She had her back to the door, but opened her eyes. It was still dark. She stretched out a hand and switched on the light so Pip should not bump into anything, but needed just another minute to come to. She closed her eyes, settling down again, but pulled back the bedcovers. 'Room for a small one, sweetie,' she addressed Pip drowsily. 'Come on in.'

'I'm not sure you truly mean that,' answered an all-male voice—and Leyne, her eyes shooting open, nearly went into heart failure!

Not believing her senses, she jerked upright, still disbelieving as she looked at the tall man standing there. 'Jack!' she gasped, struggling to get herself together. 'What time is it?' He did not have to answer; she was already reaching for her watch. It was after six. 'What's happened?' she asked. And, suddenly rapidly awake, 'Pip!' she cried. And was already swinging her long shapely legs clear of the bedclothes, ready to sprint to her.

'Nothing's happened and Pip's fine,' he answered calmly—and Leyne stared at him.

A few seconds later she had got herself sufficiently together to realise that while Jack, plainly an early riser, was up and dressed, she was sitting there in her pyjama shorts with their matching camisole top, and was showing off a long, long length of bare leg—almost up to her hip.

'Ooh!' she gasped, as his eyes appreciatively followed her line of eye.

'A very nice "Ooh",' he remarked with a grin. 'Get back in,' he suggested.

Leyne required no second bidding, and hastily dug her feet under the bedclothes, while Jack bent and brought the covers up to her waist. By which time she was more than fully *compos mentis*.

'Did I forget our appointment?' she queried, solemn-faced. She had no idea what he thought he was doing in her bedroom at this hour in the morning, but—

'Forgive me.' He cut into her thoughts. 'I've been trying to get you alone to have a word where Pip couldn't overhear. I didn't get the chance yesterday,' he added, to put a nail in the coffin of any thought Leyne may have had that he had been disappointed last night that she had refused his offer of a nightcap.

'You're going to tell her that you're her father!' she exclaimed in a rush, momentarily panicking.

'You can forget that idea!' he answered sharply, took a controlling breath, and asked, 'What's being done about her asthma?'

'Done?' Leyne queried. 'Nothing's being done!'

'Has she seen a consultant—a specialist?'

'Thank you for your concern!' Leyne retorted sharply. 'She doesn't need to see a specialist.'

'Her general practitioner is handling her case?'

'He has done from the beginning.'

Jack looked sceptical. 'He's qualified to cope with her treatment?'

'Don't come the heavy-handed father with me!' Leyne erupted, feeling at enough of a disadvantage sitting there in her nightclothes while he was fully dressed, without his questioning her medical care of his daughter.

Jack Dangerfield was unmoved. 'Is he?' he demanded.

'Yes, he is!' she tossed back. 'Apart from a physician's general experience, he has a son Pip's age with the same problem. Should there be any new or better medication on the market, he will know about it. And,' she added, feeling spleenish all of a sudden, 'if you're intending to stay around to find out his qualifications, where he qualified, his name and where he lives, would you mind sitting down somewhere? You're giving me neck-ache!'

'Did I mention that you appear to wake up in quite the most foul of tempers?' he asked mildly—and she could have crowned him.

Especially when he did no more than decide to sit on the edge of her bed. Hastily Leyne moved her legs out of the way. She hadn't meant that he should avail himself of a seat on her bed—and he was sitting much too close up—but it seemed petty to argue about it.

'So,' he took up, 'what's his prognosis?'

'That she'll grow out of it, probably when she's

about fourteen,' Leyne replied, feeling a bit fluttery in her heart region all of a sudden, and deciding to answer everything Jack wanted to know the sooner to get rid of him. 'Apart from yesterday's bout, she is already showing signs of doing so.'

'Yesterday's attack,' he said, 'was it a very bad one?'

Leyne shook her head. 'No,' she told him honestly. And less antagonistically went on, 'And her bouts are becoming less and less frequent, so I'm hopeful that Dr Haynes is right with his prognosis.'

'Is there a trigger?' Jack asked.

'Something in particular that triggers an attack, you mean?' He nodded. 'It can be anything,' Leyne replied, explaining, 'Exercise—as in running around throwing a stick for a dog. The cold weather getting onto her chest. She might be feeling quite a bit emotional too at the moment.'

'Emotional as in wanting to know who her father is?' Jack questioned, his green eyes serious on hers.

'I think so,' Leyne had to agree. And, reading what she thought was regret in his look, 'I'm sorry,' she added, with no clear idea why she was apologising—other than he looked as though Pip, his blood relationship with her, Pip's asthma, and everything about the whole of it was getting to him. A moment of sensitivity for him smote her. Poor Jack. He had been going along quite happily and then, quite out of the blue, she had hit him with this—and he couldn't even remember ever having had a brief affair with her sister twelve years ago. 'Don't be upset,' Leyne said softly, and instinctively stretched out a hand and touched his arm in a moment of empathy.

A second later she came to her senses to remember that—hang on a tick—Jack was the villain of the piece here! But even as she went to snatch her hand back, Jack had caught a hold of it and was raising it to his lips.

Shattered at his gesture, her insides somersaulted like crazy and Leyne stared at him. 'Can I have my hand back, please?' she asked witlessly, her voice gone all husky on her.

Jack's mouth quirked upwards and she had a dreadful feeling that he knew exactly how she was feeling. But he let go her hand—though only so he could place his hands on her shoulders. Then, while Leyne was still staring at him mesmerised, his hands burning into her skin that was virtually naked apart from the thin straps of her camisole top, Jack drew her gently to him and oh, so tenderly, he kissed her.

She was still staring at him stunned when he pulled back and looked into her face. 'Forgive me. I couldn't resist that,' he apologised, without managing to look in the least sorry.

'What did I do to deserve it?' she asked, her voice hopelessly lacking the acid she had been hoping for.

'I wouldn't know where to start,' he murmured, and started to move nearer again. 'You smell a sleepy kind of exquisite,' he said. And, as if wanting to know her body perfume again, at close quarters, he drew her to him and held her close up to him once more. 'Exquisite and all warm and cuddleworthy,' he said in her ear.

And Leyne laughed. 'Well, don't go overboard, Mr Dangerfield,' she ordered.

He pulled back, his green-eyed gaze taking in every detail of her face. 'Oh—come here,' he breathed—and before Leyne knew it she was in his arms, and he was not limiting his embrace to just a cuddle.

His kissed her once. She did not resist. In fact she felt then that she was incapable of resisting. When he kissed her a second time she felt in need of finding her balance, and moved her hands to his waist. His kiss deepened, and Leyne had never been kissed quite like it. She clutched at him—he kissed her a third time.

And all at once Leyne was responding. Her arms went round him, and as he drew her closer so her heart started hammering. She wanted more. As he pressed her to him, so she pressed into him, a fire shooting wildly in her as his arms and hands caressed her back.

A moment of sanity tried to get through. 'This isn't a very good idea,' she managed chokily, but knew that she did not want to use her lips for talking. She kissed him.

'Leyne!' He breathed her name. 'It isn't,' he agreed with her, and kissed her, and sent flames of wanting rocketing through her body when, with gentle hands, he caressed to the front of her and up to her breasts.

Oh, mother, she thought shakily—and closed her eyes and hung on. She was over her moment of panic a second or two later, and put her hands up over his broad shoulders, clasping her hands at back of his neck.

'You're fantastic,' he breathed, and, if that was not enough to tip her world sideways, the feel of his hands beneath her camisole top caused her to clutch on to him again.

When Jack's hands caressed to the bare skin of her breasts, Leyne felt as if she was at a crossroads. She knew she should stop this now, before it went any further. Against that, she did not want to stop it. Jack's magical touch, caressing, moulding, sensitive at the swollen globes of her breasts, and gently teasing at the hardened nub, was causing her all sorts of problems.

She gave an involuntary cry of pure pleasure. But tried again for sanity. 'Jack,' she said huskily.

'What, little darling?' he enquired in her ear.

With his caress moulding so infinitely gently at her breasts, she was having a difficult time in concentrating on conversation. 'I think,' she began, felt his fingertips caress the hard peak of her left breast, and swallowed. 'I really, really think,' she went on, striving hard to think what she did think, 'that we should— ooh…' she sighed '…we should stop right now.'

'You're right, of course,' he said, and kissed her again.

'Jack,' she said, a shade of panic entering her tones as he removed one hand from her breast, but only to begin to investigate the inside of her pyjama shorts. 'Now,' she said while she still could. 'Now, Jack!' she said more sharply—and gave him a small push away.

He instantly took his hands from her, but when she feared he might be put out that she had let matters go this far before deciding no, he was nothing of the sort. But, pulling a short way from her, he looked into her flushed face, into her need-filled, wanting, lovely blue eyes and teased, actually teased, 'You're admitting you've come over all—peculiar?'

Bravely she held his look. 'I've—um—never felt like this before,' she unthinkingly huskily admitted—and was left staring at him when he jerked further back from her.

'You're not—?' He broke off, but only to rephrase his question. 'Are you saying that you've never before—um—gone—this far?'

She gave a small nervous cough. 'Er—what self-respecting girl would admit to anything so shaming?' she evaded.

He looked shaken. 'You haven't!' he pronounced.

'I'm every man's worse nightmare,' she accepted.

'Good Lord!' he muttered.

'Don't worry about it,' she said, feeling a bit of a misfit, but trying to overcome the feeling. 'I'll know it when the moment is right.'

'But...' he still seemed a trifle stunned '...this isn't the right moment?'

It is, it is, she wanted to cry. 'I'll—er—know when,' she replied—and they both heard a sound over by the door.

Pip, her current book in her hands, stood there. 'Can I come in?' she asked.

'Please do,' Jack invited, going on, to Leyne's astonishment, 'I just popped in to give your Aunt Leyne a good-morning kiss.'

'Aunt!' Pip giggled, having never called Leyne 'Aunt' in her life, the fact that her said aunt was sitting there all rosy-cheeked passing her by.

She came over to the bed, and Jack stood and moved a little away, 'I'd better go and cook the cornflakes,' he told Pip, smiled a giving smile to Leyne, and left them to it.

Leyne did not know if she was glad or sorry that Pip was soon deeply absorbed in her book. With nothing to take her mind from her thoughts, Leyne had too much to think about.

It was no good wondering what on earth had come over her. She knew what had come over her—and it just would not do. Which was why she decided that the weekend had gone on long enough.

'I think we should make tracks for home after breakfast,' she informed Pip, coming back into the room after her shower.

'Can we take a walk on the beach first?' Pip asked, saving Leyne from having to follow through with the excuse she had ready—that she thought it better not to outstay their welcome.

'We'll see,' Leyne answered. And, unconsciously borrowing Jack's name for Pip, 'It might be an idea to go and have your shower now, poppet.'

She could have bitten her tongue, but Pip seemed not to notice, and Leyne left the bedroom some ten minutes later, knowing that she could not possibly avoid seeing Jack Dangerfield again.

She found him in the kitchen, grilling bacon. But her stomach was in such knots that she could not fully appreciate the appetising smell.

Jack turned, observed her blush as she recalled their intimate embrace, and smiled understandingly, but did not allude to it. Not just then, at any rate. 'I thought we might enjoy bacon sandwiches for breakfast,' he commented easily.

'Jack, I…' she began, and faltered.

'Jack—you?' he encouraged.

'I don't know what sort of plans you have for today,' she said in a rush, 'but I'd quite like to leave—that is, go back home—after breakfast.'

He stared at her, his clever green eyes not missing a thing about her. He switched off the grill and came over to her. Don't touch me, don't touch me, she willed, knowing she would forfeit her backbone if he so much as laid one wonderful finger on her.

He did not touch her, but halted a step or two from her. 'I've scared you—scared you away?'

'No. Not at all,' she answered honestly. She had not been scared. In his arms she had not been scared at all. It was only afterwards, when sanity and cold reason had stormed in, that she'd known that she had to put some distance between them. 'The thing is,' she explained, a little less honestly, 'I have quite a few things I must do at home—'

'Like getting Pip's clothes ready for school tomorrow?' he cut in to suggest, clearly not ready to believe her. But he remained quiet, gentle too, when he continued, 'I apologise if I went too far earlier. I confess I hadn't expected you to be so—inexperienced.' And, with a wry smile, 'How about if I forget, or try to forget, what a very tempting woman you are, and give my word to not attempt to kiss you again today while we're here?'

Out of all he had said—his apology, his word not to kiss her again while they were at Sherbourne— it was the fact that Jack thought her 'a very tempting woman' that made her speechless.

'It—er—isn't just that,' she managed, when she had the power of speech back. 'And I know our being here this weekend is more—well, all actually,' she added speedily, 'about you getting to know

Pip a little. But, don't you see? Things are complicated enough as it is, without them being added to.'

'You mean—?'

'You know what I mean,' Leyne cut in woodenly.
'You were my sister's lover, are her daughter's
father. The last thing I want to start with you, Jack,
is an affair.'

'Ouch!' he said. 'They don't come any more mis-
guided than that. You're entirely wrong, Leyne.'

'How?' she demanded, and waited for him to
repeat his assertion that he was not Pip's father and
that he had never met Max.

For once, he did not deny it. But what he did say
was even more defeating. 'You're wrong, Leyne, if
you assume that I want an affair with you,' he
replied. And, not sparing her blushes, 'As a matter
of fact, to have an affair with you is the *last* thing
on my mind.'

Embarrass me to death, why don't you? How she
kept herself from crumbling, Leyne did not know,
but somehow she did. And her tone for once was
beautifully off-hand as she managed an uppity-
sounding, 'Well, thank goodness for small mer-
cies.' And, all in the same breath, 'Do you need any
bread slicing?'

'You're one hell of a woman, Rowberry,' he
muttered as she walked by him to where the bread
was kept.

Leyne was glad to hear the sound of Pip

coming to look for them. Over bacon sandwiches and coffee, Leyne asked if it would be possible to stop off for a walk on the beach on the way back to Surrey.

'I should think so,' Jack replied, adding, with a teasing glance to Pip, 'But if Mabel's around, *I'll* throw the sticks.'

Pip laughed—and Leyne adored them both.

All too soon the weekend was over, and Jack was escorting them and their weekend bags indoors. 'Would you like coffee or something else to drink before you go?' Leyne asked, an ache already beginning within her that he would soon be gone—and she had no idea when she might see him again.

'No, thanks,' he declined. 'Things to do.' He bent down to Pip. 'Bye, poppet,' he said, and kissed her cheek. And, while Pip held a hand to her cheek as if she would never wash that spot again, Jack turned to Leyne. For several long seconds he looked into her big blue eyes, then bent his head. 'Boyfriend's privilege,' he murmured close to her ear, and before Leyne could do anything about it he gently, and just a touch lingeringly, laid his lips against hers. 'See you,' he said, and was gone. And Leyne found that as Pip had held her cheek after he had kissed it, so she had her hands to her mouth.

'You really, really like him, don't you, Leyne?' Pip asked as they walked along the hall.

'Er—I do,' Leyne answered, unable to see, with

Pip believing he was her boyfriend, how she could say anything else.

'Do you—um—love him, Leyne?' Pip asked seriously as they entered the sitting room.

Oh, sweetheart. What could she say? 'I think it's time young ladies with a too-enquiring mind should go out into the hall, pick up their weekend bag and then nip upstairs and put their belongings away,' was what she did say.

Pip laughed delightedly, not a bit put off. 'You do!' she chortled as she cheerfully danced out of the room.

And wasn't that a fact! Leyne stared after her—it was true. She, Leyne Rowberry, was head over heels in love with Jack Dangerfield. She loved him so much it hurt. So much did she love him that it had not seemed at all alien to hold him, and to want him to hold her and caress her that morning. Indeed, right now, she felt a burning hunger to be held by him, a burning need to have him caress that ache of love away.

But the simple fact was that, while Jack was not averse to a bit of early-morning dalliance, by no means did he want a fully-fledged affair with her.

And, of course, she was very pleased about that!

CHAPTER SIX

THOUGHTS of Jack Dangerfield dominated her head on and off throughout what was pretty much a sleepless night. How she had come to fall in love with him she had not the remotest idea. But love him she did.

As her sister before her had fallen for him, so too had she. But that must be an end to it—even though Leyne instinctively knew that her feelings for Jack Dangerfield were there to stay. Already her love for him felt rooted. But, while she might be a 'very tempting woman', neither she nor Jack wanted an affair. So goodbye to all that.

And yet, even as she left her bed on Monday morning and was occupied in getting ready for the day, Leyne knew a yearning to be held by him. He need not kiss her, just hold her, hold her close. That was all she would ask.

With five minutes to spare before they left the house to go and pick up Alice, Leyne checked that

Pip had everything she would need for the day.
'Better put your coat on, Pip,' Leyne suggested—
and heard Pip's gasp of dismay.

'I left it in Jack's car!' she wailed.

And that was when Leyne became conscious that
yesterday, with the discovery of her love for Jack
so new, and with thoughts of him so filling her
head, she had missed noticing that Pip's coat was
not hanging up in the cloakroom.

'You—'

'I took it off—when we came off the beach and
Jack turned the car heater up!' Pip explained. 'I
took it off when I got warm.'

'I should have noticed when I checked we'd got
everything.' Leyne attempted to ease Pip's panic.

'It must have fallen off the back seat onto the floor!'

Oh, grief. 'You'll have to wear mine.'

'I can't! I'll get into trouble for not wearing my
school uniform!'

'I'll write you a note to give to Miss Jameson,'
Leyne said, sounding calmer than she felt—now
she was going to have to contact Jack! He obviously
hadn't spotted Pip's topcoat either.

'I can wear my blazer,' Pip tried.

'It will be all right sweetheart. It's too cold for
just a blazer, and with a bit of luck we'll have your
coat back by tomorrow.'

'Will you ring Jack?'

'I'll ring Jack,' Leyne assured her. And, with that

small crisis dealt with, she went to the bureau to write Pip's teacher a note, found one of the many spare inhalers and popped it into the pocket of the topcoat Pip was now wearing, and said, 'Ready?'

Never had Leyne felt so dithery. She thought it would be pointless ringing Jack before nine, so left it until she was in her office to make the call. Yet many minutes passed before she could bring herself to do so.

Starting to feel extremely impatient and cross with herself, Leyne snatched up the phone and dialled his business number. Things were looking up, she discovered, when very shortly she was put through to him.

'Leyne!' His voice was welcoming. 'Missing me?' he couldn't resist asking.

So much. She had seen him only yesterday—it seemed ages ago. 'In your dreams!' she scoffed, and launched straight in, feeling all weak and vulnerable just from hearing his voice. 'The thing is, Pip left her topcoat in the back of your car and—'

'Does she have another?' he cut in. As Leyne had thought, he had not spotted Pip's coat on the floor at the rear of his car either.

'She's gone to school wearing a coat of mine, but I wondered if...'

'I'll drive over to her school and drop it in to her,' he said straight away. 'Does she have a spare inhaler?'

'Oh, Jack,' Leyne said helplessly. 'You'd have made a wonderful father.'

'I'll let you know when,' he answered lightly.

Leyne wasn't quite sure what to make of that comment, so decided to be more businesslike. 'There's no need for you to drive over to Pip's school. She has several spare inhalers, and she'll be all right with my coat for today.' It did not fit her, but at least it kept the cold off her chest. 'I know how busy you must be, but if you could retrieve her coat for me, I'll pick it up from your reception area in my lunch hour.'

As she had thought, he was a busy man, and did not stop to argue. 'I'll see to it,' he assured her—and that was the end of it.

Leyne, feeling all shaky inside afterwards, was unable to concentrate on her work for quite some minutes. She left her desk and headed to the ladies' room. She passed Keith Collins on the way; he ignored her. It worried her not.

Jack, and the prospect of going to his place of work, fidgeted at her for the rest of the morning. So much so she arranged to bring her lunch hour forward an hour. She left her office on the dot of twelve, wanting this errand done and out of the way. No sooner did she have Pip's coat in her car than she could start to unwind.

It proved to be not so simple. The coat had not been left at reception for her to collect! Realising that

Jack, busy as she had supposed, had not yet found time to check out the rear of his car, Leyne guessed that he'd thought he had until one o'clock to do so.

Blaming her inner agitation that she had not foreseen that possibility when she had changed her lunch hour, Leyne, aware that she had upwards of an hour to kill, was about to turn away from the reception desk when the receptionist said, 'Mr Dangerfield requested that you were shown up to his office when you arrived.'

Leyne opened her mouth ready to state that that was not necessary when a weakness to see him vanquished any such notion. Instead she smiled at the receptionist, smiled at the security guard who came over when called and, with her heart racing, went with the man to where the lifts were.

Perhaps she wouldn't see him, she pondered as the lift rose upwards. Perhaps she would be shown into his PA's office and would find that Jack had left Pip's coat there.

Leyne's heart was still drumming wildly when the security man escorted her along a corridor, knocked on one of the doors, and opened it for her.

'Leyne!' Jack was already on his feet and coming towards her. He appeared unsurprised to see her, and she realised the receptionist must have rung him to say she was on her way. 'Come in,' he invited as the security man went away closing the door behind him.

'I'm sorry to have to interrupt your day,' she apologised.

'Think nothing of it,' he answered charmingly. 'I was going to contact you anyway.'

Her eyes widened a little. 'You were?' Was he ready to let Pip know that he was her father?

Jack nodded. 'I was thinking that you and I might have dinner one evening.'

He was asking her out on a date? Her heartbeats went into overdrive. That was when Leyne knew she was either going to have to use logical thinking common sense, or crumple in a heap at his feet.

'Why?' she asked coolly. He knew what she wanted to hear—that he was ready to admit to Pip that he was her father—she did not have to dine with him *à deux* for that.

'Why not?' he countered.

Her legs felt weak. She searched for, and found, a modicum of backbone. 'I cannot see any good reason to have dinner with you,' she informed him, proud of her aloof tone—even if her heart was beating nineteen to the dozen.

He smiled, a smile so devastating, so full of charm, that her backbone was water again. 'You don't like me?' he questioned soulfully.

Stop it, stop it. I adore you. 'I don't have to like you!' she retorted snappily.

'You like kissing me.' He pulled the rug from beneath her feet.

She felt her lips twitching. She couldn't keep it up. 'Oh, shut up,' she said helplessly—and suddenly they were both laughing.

They were still looking into each other's laughing eyes when the communicating door to the next office burst open and a smartly dressed woman of about forty came in, carrying a sheaf of papers. 'Oh, sorry—didn't know you were engaged!' she exclaimed, glancing from one to the other—apart from the fact that she would have known about it, this very obviously was not a business meeting.

Since she was already in the room, she went over to the large desk and placed the papers down, and Jack introduced his PA, Yvonne Lyle.

'We've spoken on the phone,' Yvonne commented with a friendly smile. But, with her mind clearly half on business, she turned to her employer and stated, 'Talking of the phone, Noel Bridger must be burning the midnight oil. He's just rung through from Australia. I've put a note on your desk. It must be gone midnight now where he is.' She was on her way to the door when she paused to cheerfully recall, 'Though you would know better than me about their time zones.'

'You've been to Australia?' Leyne asked Jack, because she thought she should add some pleasantry—though of course she wanted to know everything she could about him, this time from the love she had for him.

'I have,' he responded in likewise pleasant manner, 'though not for some years.'

'Twelve years, to be precise,' Yvonne put in. 'Going on thirteen, to be more precise,' she added, taking a few steps towards the open communicating door.

'You've a good memory,' her employer remarked lightly, briefly, as if about to change the subject.

'I couldn't forget a thing like that,' Yvonne replied with a smile. 'I'd only just been assigned to work with you—and you disappeared over there from March to September to—'

'I'll ring Bridger shortly.' Jack cut her off. And Yvonne, obviously having a first-class working relationship with her boss, good-humouredly took the hint that he preferred to end this discussion, and disappeared back into her own office.

'Your PA seems very pl—' Leyne began lightly as the door closed—but she came to an abrupt stop, what Yvonne had just said lingering in her head. It started to puzzle her, though she had not a clue why. Until suddenly what Yvonne Lyle had said all at once began to take on a new and mortifying shape. And, as an avalanche of shock began to cascade about Leyne's head, so she stared at Jack in open-mouthed stupefaction.

'Leyne…' he said.

But she was not listening to anything but the incredible jumble in her head that was trying to make the craziest sense. 'She said…' Leyne couldn't finish it. The hairs on her nape were standing on end as what the PA had just said took on some quite colossal meaning. Stunned, and with her eyes saucer-wide, Leyne could not take her eyes off him as, still not quite believing it, she began to take in what her brain—with its aptitude for numbers—was trying to tell her.

Jack had been in Australia from March to September twelve years ago; Max had never *been* to Australia! 'You were—out of the country from March to September twelve years ago?' Leyne put her thoughts into words, while trying to deny the insisting logic of her head. Jack did not answer. But this was too important, much too important for Leyne to leave it there. 'I'll take that as a yes, then,' she said stonily. And, pushing further ahead, no sign of laughter about either of them now, 'Did you stay in Australia the whole of that time?' she insisted on knowing.

Again it looked as if he would not answer, but Leyne had the bit between her teeth, and by no chance was she going to yield. And after long moments of just looking at her and saying nothing, he at last conceded, 'That was the idea.'

'You did not once during that time come home?'

'Look, we need not go into this now.'

'Did you or didn't you?' she demanded, in shock still.

He did not care for her tone; she could tell that.

But, albeit reluctantly, 'No,' he answered, and confirmed, 'I went in March and did not return until September.' Leyne felt herself lose some of her colour. 'Leyne, I…' he began, and took a step towards her.

She took as step back, and he halted. 'Pip was conceived in July,' she said, her voice fading. She swallowed hard. 'While you were in Australia!' She just could not leave it there, but had almost completely lost her voice when she brought out that which she simply could not fail to see. 'You are not Pip's father!' she exclaimed on a hoarse note of sound. 'You can't possibly be,' she whispered, and as he moved to come forward again she took another step back, striving with her stunned senses to get her head together. And as everything snapped into place, her colour went from the very pale of shock to a furious red—of embarrassment. 'You said you weren't—and I wouldn't believe you!'

She couldn't take it. She turned and headed blindly for the door. But, moving fast, Jack was there before her. 'I—' he tried, halting her, but she was not ready to listen.

'That DNA test…' She was struggling and knew it. 'You—lied?' she accused, and blamed her head that she could not see one possible reason why he should lie about a matter of such importance. 'You said that Pip is related to you by blood, but—'

'I told you the truth,' Jack interrupted her. 'I

believe Pip and I are related—there was sufficient DNA to prove that much.'

Leyne still did not know if she should believe him. 'But you're not her father!' she said, more to herself than to him, more as if trying to get that information established in her head.

'No,' he confirmed evenly, 'I know I am not her father.'

'You said you had never met Max.' She was floundering and searching for something concrete, something solid, while all she had thought and believed was collapsing about her.

'I haven't.'

Her head was spinning. But, having gone through a whole welter of emotions in the last few minutes, shock and embarrassment to name but two, Leyne was suddenly furiously angry. 'Well—if I'm to believe you about that DNA result—*somebody* of your blood knows my sister!' she flared. And, too angry to even begin to think of backing down, 'Who?' she demanded.

Jack held her angry look, but—oddly it seemed to her then—he appeared to be torn in two. 'I—can't tell you,' he replied quietly.

And that knocked her sideways. 'Can't—or won't?' she snapped furiously. But—as shock, embarrassment, love and fury all fused together—her world seemed to fall apart. She could not take any more. Without another word she turned speedily about and crashed out of there. This time he did not try to prevent her from leaving.

Leyne was back at her office without having the least memory of how she had got there. All along he had known he was not Pip's father. And all along she had pushed and pushed at him to admit that he was. Leyne felt herself flushing again. Oh, the humiliation, the mortification of it!

Minute after minute went by as Leyne tried to come to terms with the utter fool she had made of herself.

Then all at once she was surfacing, to start to stretch her thoughts outwards. And, hang on a moment here. She took a steadying breath, and then began to give thought to what their weekend at Sherbourne had been all about. Jack had wanted to get to know Pip, so he had said. But why? He wasn't her father! He had said so many times.

Too late now to wish she had believed him! Leyne sifted through a whole welter of other things Jack Dangerfield has said, asked and answered. From the very first he had declined to believe he had a daughter. From the very first he had denied ever knowing her sister!

Suddenly his question, that first time he had come to their home, of had her sister ever been to Australia, made sense. He had been certain that he had never been her sister's lover. He had known he had been in Australia at the time of Pip's conception. The fact that Max had never been to that continent had merely confirmed what he already knew anyway. He had never, as he had said, met the lady.

With her thoughts in turmoil, it was only then that Leyne realised that, with her head in a whirl, she had rocketed out from Jack's office so fast she had left without the very object of her visit in the first place. She had charged out of there without Pip's coat!

Well, she wasn't going back for it! That was for certain. That meant that her only alternative was to take an hour off work and, bother the expense, go and buy Pip a new coat. This was no time for logic, which wanted to point out that the missing coat had been new at the start of Pip going to her senior school in September.

Leyne was about to go and see Tad Inglefield about some time off, when the door opened and Tad himself walked in. He was carrying Pip's coat!

'Where did you get that?' she exclaimed, her insides on the churn again—had Jack brought it over?

'I was in Reception when a messenger handed it in.'

Leyne thanked Tad, mentioning that her niece had left it somewhere.

By the time Leyne left her office at the end of her working day, although still feeling embarrassed whenever she thought of what had transpired that lunchtime—and she thought of it constantly—she was much calmer. And by that time she had been able to think more clearly, and was able to search further into her realisation that, with Jack being certain that there was sufficient DNA to establish that he and Pip were related in some way, and since clearly he was not Pip's father, then someone else in his family must be the culprit.

He knew who it was too. But was he saying? Was he blazes! Leyne drove to pick up her niece wondering who. She had an idea Jack was an only child—so who? Some cousin, perhaps? Some cousin who without a doubt had led Max to believe he was the chairman of J. Dangerfield, Engineers. Some cousin whom Jack Dangerfield was plainly protecting.

Well, he need not bother, she fumed sniffily. They wanted nothing from him or his cousin. Sadly, though, Pip deserved better. She was the loveliest child, and to Leyne it seemed little short of criminal that Pip's father should refuse to acknowledge her.

When the phone rang that night Leyne's thoughts immediately shot to Jack. Ridiculous. She would not be hearing from him again. Not that she wanted to. Pip was in the bath. Leyne, hoping against hope that it would be Max—she had such a lot to tell her—sped to answer it.

It was not Max, nor was it Jack Dangerfield. It was, in fact, Ben Turnbull—Max's highly esteemed photographer employer!

'Max has been very anxious to contact you—' he began.

'She's all right?' Leyne cut in quickly, instantly wondering why he was phoning and not her sister.

'She's fine,' he assured her, but admitted, 'Max has been ill,' adding, before Leyne should be too alarmed, 'But she is making a very good recovery.'

'What's wrong with her? Where is she?' Leyne's questions were thick and fast, but Ben Turnbull was able to answer every one of them.

It appeared that Max had cut her leg and had neglected to tell anyone about it. The cut had gone 'bad ways', which had led to complications, and before long she had developed a fever and become delirious.

'Delirious?' Leyne exclaimed, only just holding her feelings of trepidation in check.

'She's fine now, as I said. Making rapid strides, in fact,' he assured her, going on to state how in her delirium she had feared her daughter had come to some harm. 'Nothing would do but I had to send someone to make contact with you, to check she was all right.'

'Someone named Urbano phoned,' Leyne said.

'When Max was more lucid Urbano was able to relay that he had been able to speak to her child in person.' Ben Turnbull then got to the purpose of his call. 'Max wants you to know that she is thinking of you both, and for you not to worry, and to send you and Pip the biggest hug.'

'You're sure she is going to be all right?'

'Positive,' he answered. And, his voice strangely

softer somehow, 'I would not have left her other-wise.' His voice was firmer when he said, 'Max will ring you for what she terms "a good long chat" as soon as she can. With luck, next week some time.'

Leyne's eyes felt moist as the call ended. She felt choked that, as ill as Max must have been, her thoughts and worries had been about them, in par-ticular about her daughter.

Leyne heard Pip leave the bathroom and, realis-ing if Max had been delirious that she must have been gravely ill, knew that she had to tell Pip about the phone call.

'There was a message from your mum while you were in the bath,' Leyne began.

'Oh, I missed her!' Pip cried.

'It wasn't your mum; it was her boss.'

'Ben Turnbull?'

Leyne nodded. 'Apparently, Max has been a little unwell.' Leyne downplayed her sister's illness. 'She's better now,' Leyne explained quickly, 'and will try and ring us next week. But for now she wanted Mr Turnbull to ring and say hello, and to let us know that she is thinking of us and her special darling daughter.'

Pip cheered up immediately, though was clear-thinking enough to ask, 'If Mr Turnbull could ring, why couldn't my mum?'

Leyne adopted a ghostly voice. 'Who knows?' she called from afar. It had the desired effect. Pip giggled.

It was later in the week that Leyne spotted Pip giving her 'that look' again. 'Leyne,' she said, and Leyne knew what was coming.

'Philippa?' she enquired back, teasingly.

'When my mum rings next week, will you ask her?'

'I intend to, sweetheart,' Leyne answered, not needing to ask the subject matter. 'I'm sorry, love,' she went on gently, knowing that an apology was due. 'I *have* tried to find out for you, but I've— um—hit a bit of a brick wall.'

'That's all right,' Pip said sweetly. 'I just know that you'll try your very best.'

Leyne remembered what her niece had said when, midway through Friday morning, the phone on her desk rang and, to her astonishment, she heard Jack Dangerfield ask charmingly, 'How's the most beautiful woman on the planet?'

'You've got a nerve!' she snapped pithily, even as her heart played its usual skippy beat to hear him.

'What did I do?' he enquired, all innocence.

'You don't *know*?'

'All I did was tell you I was not Pip's father. It's not my fault if you didn't believe me,' he pointed out—quite fairly, she recognised.

But she did not want to be the one put in the wrong here. 'You've known all along who her father is—' she hissed.

'I've suspected who he is,' he cut in.

'Suspected?'

'I only received confirmation last night,' he replied.

'Confirm... You *know* now who he is?'

'I do.'

Her heartbeats were still racing. 'Do I get to know who? For myself, I wouldn't give a button, but Pip still wants to know.'

'Of course she does,' he agreed, which put Leyne totally out of her stride.

'You're—prepared to tell me his name?' she asked, holding her breath.

'I am,' he answered. 'This weekend.'

'This weekend!' Leyne echoed.

'There's a lot to explain. I thought we'd go down to Sherbourne tonight, then—'

'Oh, no!' she cut in sharply.

'Oh, come on, Leyne. I'd much rather discuss this face to face—and it wasn't so very terrible last weekend while we were there. Was it?'

In a flash she was reliving those heady moments in his arms last Sunday. 'I—er...' she mumbled huskily.

And realised he had either been reading her mind, or that he was thinking the self-same thing, because, his voice all coaxing, 'As I remember it, Pip made a splendid chaperone,' he murmured.

'I—er...' Leyne said again. But Jack reminding her of Pip had set her thinking of how her niece had so trustingly said 'I just know that you'll try your very best'. Was it her best to refuse to co-operate with Jack? 'Same time as last Friday,' she agreed, and before he could answer, before she should change her mind, Leyne slammed down the phone.

Pip positively beamed when Leyne relayed the news that they would be spending a second weekend at Sherbourne, and that Jack would be calling for them shortly. 'Great!' she exclaimed. But, shortly after that, 'I need some art materials for school on Monday!' she said anxiously. 'I was going to ask if we could go and get them tomorrow.'

'Well, I expect, if we both behave ourselves, that Jack might take us into the nearest town tomorrow,' Leyne replied, and Pip was all smiles once again. Alice was spending the weekend with her father, so Leyne had no need to cancel the standing swimming arrangement.

Both she and Pip were ready when Jack's car pulled up on the drive. But by then Leyne had recalled how he had tried, and succeeded, in entirely bamboozling her into believing that he, as a 'maybe' father, had more right with Pip than her—when he had known full well that he jolly well hadn't.

Leyne tried to maintain a reserved front, but found it difficult. She loved the wretched man, was in love with him, and, regardless what her outward expression might be saying, it was pure and utter joy just to be with him.

Pip had greeted him a little shyly, but he made

short work of her initial shyness and they were soon chatting away like old chums.

'Let's see what Mrs Ford has prepared for us,' he said when they arrived at Sherbourne. And, dropping their bags down in the hall, they went to investigate in the kitchen.

Time was going on by the time they had done justice to the excellent casserole Mrs Ford had left for them. Leyne allowed Pip to help with the clearing away after their meal. But once the dishwasher had been stacked and was underway, it was way past her normal bedtime, and even though there was no school tomorrow, Leyne suggested it was time that all growing young ladies were tucked up in bed.

'All right if I read for a while?' Pip asked as Leyne went up the stairs with her.

'Certainly it is. I'll pop in and turn your light off if you fall asleep reading.'

'You're going back downstairs again?' Pip asked, probably remembering how the previous Friday Leyne had stayed upstairs with her.

'I thought I might.'

Pip grinned. 'Well, Jack *is* your boyfriend.'

Leyne saw Pip settled, but knew in her head that she was not going to settle herself until she had heard all there was to hear. No way was she going to leave it until tomorrow.

Leyne made her way down the stairs with concern for her niece uppermost. Whatever happened, whatever Jack had to explain—and there was a lot to explain he had said—she was not going to allow Pip to be hurt. Should what he have to say reveal that the man Max had once loved was some kind of villain, then Leyne knew she would tread very carefully about what she would tell Pip. The child deserved honesty, that was true enough. Against that, though, Pip was not yet twelve years old, and Leyne would guard with all she had that she be told only as much as any eleven-and-a-half-year-old could be expected to handle.

She made for the drawing room—and found Jack there waiting for her. Clearly, he knew why she had returned downstairs. Leyne turned about and firmly closed the door. She had no wish for what they had to discuss to be overheard should Pip wander down for any reason.

'Would you like something to drink?' Jack enquired courteously, on his feet and coming forwards.

'No, thank you,' she replied. She was his guest; she would stay pleasant—for now.

'Come and sit down,' he invited.

Feeling very nervous suddenly, Leyne went over to one of the several padded armchairs in the room. Jack took one opposite. They looked at each other. For long moments green eyes looked into blue ones, and for long seconds Leyne forgot what this was all about.

But she gave herself a mental shake. This would never do! 'You—um—said—you said that last night you had confirmation of whom you suspected was Pip's father?' she opened, feeling very anxious about what she was about to hear.

'That's true. From—comments you'd made, I was fairly certain I knew,' Jack replied. 'But—there were—are—complications.'

'You're not trying to wriggle out of telling me? Not now!' Leyne fired shortly.

'Wriggle out?' he challenged toughly.

She refused to apologise. That was the purpose of them being here—so Jack could explain the 'lot' he had to explain. 'Can we cut to the chase?' she asked coldly.

'You want to know who Pip's father is?'

She gave him a sharp look. 'We've established that you are not her father—despite your claim, when it suited you, that as her maybe father you had more right than her unofficial guardian!' Leyne told him waspishly.

He smiled. It killed her antagonism stone-dead. 'I'm a terrible person,' he said, with such charm she just could not prevent her lips from twitching.

'So?'

'So,' he took up, 'I last night had dinner with the man I was by then next to certain—against my initial incredulity—was Pip's father. I had asked him to meet me on a matter of some importance.'

Leyne was feeling tense again. 'You asked him outright if he was...?'

Jack shook his head. 'I didn't have to. What I did ask was if he had ever heard of a woman named Maxine Nicholson.'

'He said that he had?

'He was a bit startled by the question. I think he'd thought that when I'd said I would like to see him on an important matter, that it was to be something to do with business. Anyhow, he said that he had known Maxine, but that had been some years ago. When I then asked him if he knew that Maxine had a daughter who would be twelve next April, it didn't take him long to work out the maths.' Jack paused reflectively, and then revealed, 'He went from looking startled to being absolutely staggered.'

'He had no idea about Pip?'

'He was speechless!' Jack stated.

'But he admitted he might be Pip's father?'

'I didn't even have to suggest that he might be.'

'He accepted straight away, without you having to—?'

'Straight away,' Jack cut in. 'Despite what you might have thought, he is an honourable man. He had only good things to say about your sister. He said how she was warm and wonderful at a time when he needed someone like her in his life. He said that Maxine was a very private kind of person and—without needing to question—that if she had become pregnant during the time he had known her, that the child was his.'

Against her will, Leyne was getting to like the sound of this man to whom Max had given her heart. Which led her to think that it was about time that she asked that all-important question. 'Who is he?' she asked quietly.

Jack eyed her steadily for a moment and then, equally quietly, he disclosed, 'He is the former chairman of J. Dangerfield.'

Leyne's eyes widened. *'Former* chairman?' she gasped. But, recovering, 'My mother got that part right.' And, because she still did not know his name, 'Who is he?' she repeated.

'Your mother got the next bit right too,' Jack said, and supplied, 'Pip's father is a man called John Dangerfield.'

'The same name as yours,' she murmured absently. 'A relative of yours?'

'My name is Jack, not John,' he told her, and, causing her eyes to go wider than ever, 'John Dangerfield is—my father.'

Tense seconds followed while what he had just said sank in. 'Your *father*—is Pip's father?' Leyne was gasping.

'He would have been around forty-eight or nine at the time.'

Leyne was in shock. 'Max was twenty-three,' she supplied, trying to get over what Jack had just told her. 'You've known, suspected, for some while?' she questioned.

'At the very start I knew I wasn't Pip's father, so there seemed to me nothing I should do.'

'You thought if you ignored me, the problem not yours, I might go away?'

'You're not so easy to ignore, Miss Rowberry,' he said lightly. 'That DNA was a shaker, I admit. But I knew when I got the result back that I just could not do nothing, for all I'd had the report some while before I took action.'

'You suspected your father might be…'

'I just couldn't believe it was him. It seemed too totally incredible to be him! Then I found I was pretty much having to concede that he must be Pip's father,' he owned, 'that night you and I had dinner and you asked was I, or was I not, John Dangerfield, chairman of J. Dangerfield, Engineers.' He paused, and then added, 'And therein lay the problem.'

'You didn't want to—put that question to him?'

'It isn't that simple.'

'It never is,' she commented stiffly.

'There isn't only my father to consider. I respect both of my parents.'

'They're divorced?'

'No.'

'Separated? Your mother…?'

'Is well.' Jack leaned a little forward in his chair to add, 'They are extremely happy together.'

'Don't let me be the one to rock the boat!' Leyne threw in, thinking of the years of unhappiness Max must have endured. Though, to be fair to John Dangerfield, by the sound of it he'd had no clue that she had been pregnant when they had broken up. And, for a marvellous compensation, that pregnancy had resulted in a wonderful daughter. 'I'm sorry,' she said, on thinking about it.

'Accepted,' he commented, and gave her one of his spine-melting smiles. 'My father wants to meet Pip,' he announced.

Leyne's reaction was instant and immediate. 'No!' she answered sharply, instinctively.

'No?'

'I—er…I need to think about it. I need to know more about him. You've only just revealed his name—we're not ready yet to—'

'I've told him how protective you are of her,' Jack cut in. 'On his part he would not dream of doing anything to harm or upset Pip. Trust me, Leyne, he *is* an honourable man…'

'It sounds like it. I presume he was married to your mother when he decided to break his marriage vows and have a—a—liaison with my sister!'

Jack tossed her a sharp look, but manfully took her remarks on the chin, and explained, 'It wasn't that clear-cut.'

'I'm sure!'

'You can be all acid at times!' Jack grated harshly.

It was true. 'But you enjoy kissing me,' she threw back at him.

He eyed her, his lips starting to twitch. 'Shut up,' he said, much the same way she had. But he was serious when he opened up, 'At the time my father met Maxine both he and my mother were having a very bad time of it.'

'Their marriage was—rocky?' Leyne queried.

Jack nodded. 'Unbeknown to me they were at that time, to all intents and purposes, separated. I had absolutely no idea—their marriage had always seemed to me to be rock-solid. Which is probably why I had such a hard time taking it in that he had—strayed.'

'You were—shaken?'

'Staggered,' Jack agreed. 'I had no idea until last night, when my father explained that prior to him meeting your sister, my mother had demanded a divorce, and had, in fact, insisted that they went their separate ways. Maxine,' he said after a moment's pause, 'happened along at just the time when my father's world had crashed around him.' Leyne looked back at Jack. He had said that there was a lot to explain. It seemed there was more. 'To go back to the beginning,' he resumed, 'my mother was horrifically injured in a riding accident, with the prognosis being that she would never be able to leave her bed, much less walk again.' Leyne stared at him, feeling shaken by what he had just said. 'This to a woman who was never still and always on the move—it sent her into a deep depression. In that state my mother set her mind on a divorce, told my father so, and thereafter refused to see him.'

'Where were you at this time—in Australia?'

'At the time of the accident, no. I delayed going for a month or so, but once we knew that there was nothing more to be done, my father was emphatic that I must go. I kept in frequent contact, of course, but each time I suggested I should come home, my father would dream up some fresh assignment to keep me there. To be honest, given my concerns about my mother, I was otherwise having a great time.'

'I'll bet,' Leyne chipped in dryly.

'I was twenty-four…'

'With some living to do.'

Jack gave her a half-smile, and went on to reveal, 'It was only last night that I learned the true reason why my father did not want me to return.'

'He didn't want you to know that he and your mother were separated and that your mother had plans to divorce him?'

'He wanted to handle what he saw as her rejection of him in his own way. No matter how close we are,' he went on, 'my father is still his own man. But it was around then—his wife hell-bent on divorce, me sent away, a time that he was feeling at his lowest—that he met Maxine. And he discovered what a sweet, sensitive and terrific person she was.'

'Did he love her?'

'He said he loved her, but in his heart he knew that he was in love with his wife. His relationship with your sister was brief, and he ended it when he started to be consumed with guilt. He faced then that, although he had feelings for Maxine, he had no stomach for the divorce he had told her looked to be how his marriage would end.'

'He ditched my sister instead.'

'Don't get uptight again,' Jack requested. 'According to my father, Maxine is as proud as she is lovely. He had the impression they parted by mutual consent. He never contacted her again. He wanted to, to check that she was all right, but—' Jack shrugged '—his first priority was to get his wife to see, as he had done, that his life would be over without her in it.' Jack broke off to underline, 'It was a tremendous shock to him, Leyne, to last night learn that he had left Maxine expecting his child. When he started to get what I'd said established in his head, he said that from what he knew of your proud sister, he could only gather that, since she had not heard another word from him, she saw no point in complicating what was already a delicate situation. It wasn't as if he was childless.'

'Max knew he already had a son and heir?'

'She did. My father never, ever lied to her.'

Leyne sighed. It seemed to her that there had been a great deal of pain all round. 'Max must have believed it was for the best not to tell him, that there was no point in letting your father know.'

'Except for the one point she overlooked,' Jack stated, and, as Leyne stared at him uncomprehendingly, 'That one day her offspring would ask, and would keep on wanting to know, "Who is my father?".'

Leyne could not argue that. She got to her feet—Jack had given her a lot to think about. 'I'd better go…'

'Are you sure you wouldn't like something to drink?' Jack was on his feet too, and it was almost as if he was reluctant for her to go. But Leyne at once realised that, with so much of what he had just explained floating about in her head, her imagination was taking over.

'No, thanks,' she refused, as he walked to the door with her. Though at the door she halted, sensitive to Jack all of a sudden. 'Your mother?' she enquired gently. 'How is she now?'

Jack's natural smile was lovely to see. 'Fit as a flea,' he replied.

'She—recovered?' Leyne asked hesitantly.

'The prognosis was not so totally gloomy as was first thought. And what with her iron will, and some very complex and extremely scary surgery, she was on her feet two years after her accident and daily astounding her doctors.'

'I'm glad,' Leyne said simply, and meant it. She had turned the doorknob and was about to open the door when, with a jolt, something new all at once struck her. 'You…' she said on a faint gasp of sound.

'Me?' Jack encouraged, looking deeply into her eyes.

'Have you yet realised that you are Pip's half-brother?'

'Oh, yes,' he said with a smile. 'I've suspected that to be the case for some while.'

'And—um—how do you honestly feel about that?' Leyne enquired.

His smile broadened. 'To be perfectly honest—I'm tickled pink to have a little sister.'

Leyne smiled; she just had to. And, with her eyes glued to his, her insides suddenly started churning over again. 'Goodnight,' she remembered to say—only to discover, as Jack stretched out and took her in his arms, that it wasn't goodnight yet.

'Did anyone ever tell you that you have the most gorgeous big baby blue eyes?' he asked softly.

'I can't remember,' she answered witlessly. And, with a dreamy half-smile, 'But I expect they must have done.'

It was all that she did manage to say, because the next she knew Jack had drawn her closer to him and his wonderful, wonderful mouth, was over hers, lingering, giving, and generous. She loved him so much, it was heaven to be in his arms, and she never wanted his kiss to stop.

But all too soon Jack, taking a firm grip on her

upper arms, was putting her away from him. 'I—um—think you had better go up to bed,' he said nicely.

Leyne grinned. By the sound of it, this riot of emotion she was feeling was mutual. 'I think perhaps I better had,' she answered. Jack opened the door and she went—she went quickly.

CHAPTER SEVEN

PIP did not come, book in hand, looking for her the
next morning. A sure sign, Leyne felt, that her niece
was feeling more secure in her weekend environment.

It had taken Leyne a long time to get to sleep last
night. Jack had been in her head then; she awoke
early just the same, and Jack was in her head again.

She smiled dreamily. He had kissed her. He was
not Pip's father. He had never had a relationship
with Maxine. There was no invisible barrier to
prevent them...

Leyne instantly reined in such thoughts and,
feeling restless suddenly, got out of bed. She had no
idea of where she had been going with that kind of
thinking, but, good heavens, the poor man had
merely kissed her. He would be staggered if he
thought she had read anything at all into what, after
all, had been nothing more meaningful to him than
a kiss of empathy of the moment. Grief, if she
wanted further proof, had she so soon forgotten how,

less than a week ago, he had declared that to have an affair with her was the last thing on his mind?

Not that she wanted an affair with him either, thank you very much. Though what she did want she could not have said. All she knew was that she loved him.

But, in any event, even supposing she ruled out one set of complications, there were loads of others. Oh, my word, yes. For a start, it was not Jack who was Pip's father, but *his* father. Now, what the Dickens was she going to do about that?

Again wishing that Max was home, one thing Leyne did know was that until she had thought this thoroughly through she was not going to let Dangerfield Senior anywhere near her niece. Even if he had stated his wish to meet her.

Leyne showered and dressed and went in search of her niece, and discovered she was up and dressed too.

'Ready for breakfast?' Leyne asked.

'I'm starving!' Pip replied, growing and unfillable.

Leyne smiled, and together they left Pip's room. They were going along the landing, however, when Leyne heard a car coming up the drive. She glanced out of the landing window, expecting to see a delivery vehicle or a mail van, but the vehicle now being driven out of her line of vision was long, sleek and elegant, and nobody's idea of a trade automobile.

She guessed Jack had heard and seen it too, because as they reached the bottom of the stairs so he came along the hall, heading for the front door.

With her insides all of a jumble just to see him, Leyne managed to keep her expression composed. But it was Pip who brightly greeted him. 'Good morning, Jack,' she trilled cheerfully.

'Good morning, Miss Philippa,' he replied teasingly, and Pip chuckled sunnily.

'You've visitors,' Leyne remarked by way of a good morning.

'Visitor singular, I believe,' he replied, and as they both halted, and he looked solemnly down into the eyes he had last night described as gorgeous, 'It's my father's car,' he stated.

'Your father!' Leyne's eyes shot wide, an arm automatically going out to draw Pip to her. But even as she acted so instinctively fury was breaking in her. 'You knew!' she accused. 'You…' She controlled herself. Had Pip not been there Leyne felt then that she might have physically lashed out at him for putting her in the position of having to allow her niece to meet this man before she had time to think about it and talk to Maxine. Well, she could soon sort that another way. 'Pip and I will go upstairs while you entertain your—' The ringing of the doorbell cut through her determination to remove her niece from even the smallest chance of harm.

But Jack was taking even that option from her when he caught hold of Pip—his sister—by the hand. 'Come and say hello to my father,' he said to her lightly. 'He'll be most offended if you run away.'

That left Leyne with few choices if she did not want to wrench Pip from him in an ungainly tug-o-war. With her first thought for her niece, and bearing in mind that she did not want the clever child to pick up any sense of a hostile atmosphere, 'We'll stay here while you answer the door,' she conceded, hostility nonetheless in her eyes that looked coldly into searching green ones—albeit that she managed to keep that hostility from her voice.

Jack took his eyes from her, let go Pip's hand and went to open the door to his father. Leyne heard them greet each other, but was more preoccupied with checking that Pip was unperturbed. Then the front door was closing and, with Jack saying, 'Come and meet Leyne and Pip,' two tall men were coming towards them.

John Dangerfield—Jack's father, Pip's father—was a handsome man. He had the Dangerfield thick black hair. The only difference were the wings of pure white at his temples. His eyes—green eyes—as he walked towards them, were solely for his daughter.

'I've brought some bacon and eggs,' he said to her, holding out the plastic carrier he had in one hand. 'Do you think I may be allowed to come to breakfast?'

Pip did not answer, but as Jack came in to perform the introductions Leyne could see that Pip was quite fascinated by the man who looked so much like Jack. His charm, too, was so much like his son's as he shook hands with Leyne and said, 'I've heard so much about you, Leyne, I hope you don't mind me calling unannounced.' Every bit as though she was the hostess here.

'Not at all,' she found herself answering quietly. His seniority deserved respect, without the fact she could not very well go charging in guns blazing with Pip an interested spectator.

Jack and his father cooked bacon and egg, leaving Leyne and Pip little to do but lay the table. In this instance of a full breakfast, they opted to eat in the dining room.

'What would you like to do this morning?' Jack asked, when they were all seated round the table.

Pip looked pleadingly to Leyne, and Leyne only then remembered that her niece was anxious about some art materials. 'Pip and I need to go into town for some art materials she needs for school on Monday,' she replied. And, not wanting to be beholden to either Dangerfield, 'We'll make our own way there.'

Jack gave her a sharp look, clearly not best pleased that she had decided to be this independent—like she cared, the angry way she was feeling just then! But it was his father who pleasantly volunteered, 'I'll take you.'

'We couldn't...'

'Of course you could,' he countered with a warm smile, obviously set on not offending her. 'Besides, it's ages since I last had chance to browse around an art shop.'

Leyne could see, as Pip looked forward to this small outing, that she was clearly impressed with Jack's father. So much so that after breakfast she helped him carry some of their used dishes out to the kitchen. Leyne could hear them chatting as Pip showed him what he should know about the dishwasher.

Jack was in the dining room as Leyne put away condiments and generally tidied. She wished he would clear off—she had nothing she wanted to say to him.

She had just reached over to pick up a place-mat when Jack snaked out a hand and caught hold of her wrist. Angrily she shook his hand away, and straightened up to scowl belligerently at him. He looked as tough as she felt, she observed.

'Hate me, but don't hate my father!' he rapped crisply.

'Well, that's easily done!' she snapped—and seemed to have oddly tweaked his sense of humour, because, from looking tough and ready to sort her out—let him try!—his face suddenly creased.

'Oh, Leyne,' he said softly. She felt herself weakening—she mustn't let that happen. 'Would you, from that wonderful warm heart of yours, do me a special favour?'

She stared at him. Of all the nerve! He presented

her with a *fait accompli*—the arrival of his father—and wanted a special favour on top! 'Lend me your joke book!' she answered—not very nicely, it had to be said.

'Let Pip go into town with my father on her own.'

'You definitely *are* joking!' Leyne flew.

'Aw, come on,' he coaxed. 'They'll be there and back in an hour.'

'No!'

'Surely you're not going to begrudge my father, *her* father, an hour with her—an hour in which to get to know her a little?'

'Yes, I am!' she was adamant.

Jack Dangerfield got tough. 'You've had the joy of knowing that delightful child for going on twelve years. Can't you trust her father with her for one measly hour?'

'It isn't that.' Drat him. Put like that, it really was weakening.

'What then?' he demanded.

'She's precious. I don't want her hurt.'

'She won't be hurt. My father will say nothing to upset Pip. I can promise you that,' Jack insisted, and, his hard tone easing, 'Haven't you seen for yourself how totally bowled over he is when looking at her unobserved? He'll guard her with his life, Leyne.'

Leyne turned her back on him and walked out of the dining room. Pip was coming merrily along from the kitchen. 'I'm just going upstairs for my coat. Shall I bring yours?' she asked.

'I'll come too,' Leyne decided. But away from Jack, away from Pip as Pip went to her own room, Jack's remark about her having had the joy of knowing Pip for going on twelve years started to sink in.

Was she being mean-spirited? An hour, that was all. An hour for John Dangerfield to get to know a little of the daughter he had never known that he had until a day and a half ago. And was she right to try and prevent him from getting to know her?

And was it up to her anyway? It seemed to Leyne then that it was quite likely that when Max came home, or before, if they ever got to have a telephone conversation, she would have no objection to make to her daughter getting to know her father.

Though, in the end, what mattered most was what was right for Pip. And, after a few minutes of deliberating, Leyne recognised the answer. On his part John Dangerfield would guard his own. Nor would he say a word that might worry or upset her, his daughter. As for Pip—what was a special hour with her father? For ages now she had not only wanted to know who he was, but also had wanted to meet him.

'Ready?' Pip called, coming to look for her.

'I've a few things I need to do. Mr Dangerfield will be pleased to take you, though,' she replied. 'I think he wants to look in the art shop too.'

'Is Jack coming?'

'I don't think so. Now, you know what you need?' Leyne asked, reaching for her purse and handing Pip the money she would require. Leyne collected her own coat and together they went down the stairs. Jack and his father were at the bottom, waiting for them. Leyne ignored Jack and addressed his father. 'Pip knows what she needs.'

'You're not coming with us?' he asked courteously.

'No, if you don't mind,' she answered.

He nodded a kind of thank you, and turned to his daughter. 'You have your inhaler?' he asked, and suddenly Leyne began to warm to him. As Jack had said, John Dangerfield—who had patently been acquainted with his offspring's asthma—would guard his new-found daughter with his life.

No sooner had they gone than Leyne, needing her own space to think her own thoughts, took off too. 'I'm going for a walk,' she told Jack shortly.

'You don't want company?'

'Got it in one!'

Under an hour later she returned, with nothing any clearer in her head than it had been. She had gone over everything that had taken place since Max had left, and the only conclusion Leyne had been able to come to was—what a time for Max to go!

Of course neither of them could have foreseen this turn of events. And Leyne fretted anew as she wondered if she could or should have done anything differently. While it was true that Max had many times commented that her sister was more like Pip's mother than she was, when it was all boiled down, Leyne knew that she was *not* Pip's mother.

That did not prevent her from acting as her mother would, Leyne mused, filled with self-doubt as she walked up the drive. There was no sign of the elder Mr Dangerfield's car, she saw. Though, on walking into the drawing room, her first question to Jack, who appeared to have been watching the drive from the window, was, 'They're not back yet?'

Before he could reply, the telephone rang. Normally Leyne would have left him to take his call in private. But she had no idea what was normal any more, and some sixth sense alerted that she might know who was calling.

She did. Having said hello into the instrument and listened for a second or two, Jack looked over to her. 'My father would like to take Pip to lunch. But if you say no, he'll bring her straight back.'

Instinctively Leyne wanted to say no. She wanted Pip back with her. She didn't know if that was a motherly feeling or an aunt's feeling—she just wanted her safe. She looked at Jack. He was not pressurising her, just standing and waiting for her to make what decision she would. Leyne hesitated, Jack's words about her having had the joy of Pip for nearly twelve years pounding in her head. Whereas his father had barely had an hour of that joy. And Pip was safe, wasn't she? Suddenly, then, Leyne knew that Pip could be nowhere safer than with her father.

Feeling choked all at once, Leyne nodded, and turned, and walked out of the room. She went upstairs, knowing that she had made the right decision but feeling slightly as if everything she had known and trusted before Max had gone on her assignment had collapsed about her ears.

In her room Leyne took off her coat and hung it up in the wardrobe. She was not ready to go downstairs again, so went to sit in the window seat, looking out. She felt out of sorts with Jack, and knew she would not leave her room again until she saw his father's car turn into the drive. Heaven alone knew how many hours away that would be.

Some fifteen minutes later, though, while she might have decided it better to deprive herself of Jack's company, it appeared that he had other ideas. Because quite unexpectedly her bedroom door opened, and Jack strolled in. When he closed the door behind him she guessed he had come for a chat.

Tough! She glanced at him, then went back to studying the drive. 'You didn't give me chance to say thank you,' he commented, his tone even.

'They're all right?' she questioned—Jack had still been on the phone to his father when she had left him to it. Jack came over and perched in the corner of the same window seat. He'd obviously read that, since she had replied at all, she was not averse to a chat. However, she was more concerned that he was sitting much too close.

'Given that Pip apparently refused point-blank to allow her father to pay for her purchases, they're getting on famously.'

Leyne almost smiled at that. 'Good,' she said.

'Good?' Jack queried.

Leyne shrugged. 'It's pleasing to know that even at Pip's tender age she innately appreciates the standards of her upbringing,' Leyne answered dully.

'Oh, Leyne,' Jack said softly. 'I know you're un-happy—'

His tone was bone-melting. 'Did you know your father intended to drive down here this morning?' she cut in pithily.

'That's an improvement!' he remarked pleasantly.

Leyne looked at him startled. 'What?'

'An hour or so ago you weren't asking if I knew, but accusing that I *did* know.'

'Did you?' she asked. He had lovely eyes, too lovely for a man, she couldn't help thinking.

He shook his head. 'I'd no idea,' he answered. But owned, 'I suppose, on reflection, I should have considered that he might. After I'd broken the news to him on Thursday, I said I thought I'd invite you and Pip down to Sherbourne this weekend when, with his permission, I would tell you everything.'

'He gave you that permission?'

'Readily. Though what I should have seen,

knowing full well he is not the kind of man who will easily sit back and await events, was that he would not leave it there. Not when he knew he had a daughter he had failed to love and provide for.'

'We don't need anything from him!' Leyne flared, but was instantly all at sixes and sevens when Jack stretched forwards and caught a warm hold of her hand.

'*You* don't,' he said gently. 'But what about him? What about Pip? My little sister obviously needs to know her father.' He had her there, Leyne had to admit. 'And from her father's point of view—and given his one lapse—he really in an honourable man, Leyne. He sorely needs to try and make amends.'

'He,' Leyne said shortly, 'is not my problem.' With her eyes still on Jack, she waited to see frost appear in his eyes at her reply. But, to her surprise, he instead smiled.

'You're saying that Pip is proving a problem?'

'No, I'm not. She isn't a problem. You know she isn't!' Leyne answered. She had wanted to sound sharp, but with Jack holding her hand she was finding it difficult to get stroppy with him. 'It's just that…'

'Just what?' he pressed, when she seemed unable to find the words she was searching for.

She hesitated. Then blurted out, 'I'm scared!'

'Scared? You? I don't bel—'

'I'm scared of doing the wrong thing.'

Jack's expression changed, became warmer

suddenly, and he stood up, pulled her to her feet. 'Oh, Leyne,' he said softly, and drew her closer to him, brushing a stray stand of fair hair back from her brow. 'From what I can gather, it's never easy being a parent.' He smiled into her eyes.

Leyne found his smile irresistible. She could not help but smile back. 'With or without these sort of complications,' she agreed.

'Are you going to let me help?'

'I'm getting there,' she mumbled, feeling quite mesmerised by him all at once. 'Pip is the important one here. We all must do what's best for her.'

'I couldn't agree more,' Jack murmured, his eyes on her eyes, his glance trailing down to her mouth.

What he saw there Leyne had no idea, but, as if taking her slightly parted lips for invitation—almost as if he found her mouth impossible to ignore—his head came down and he gently, tenderly, lingeringly kissed her.

'Oh,' she breathed when he pulled back and looked into her eyes.

'I think I feel pretty much the same,' he said lightly. Leyne smiled, and he did it again—he kissed her—this time with his arms all the away around her.

Held in the circle of his arms, Leyne tried desperately hard, as he again drew back to look into her eyes, to remember what they had been talking about. 'Of course we have to take into account what

Pip wants in all of this,' she managed, even if her voice did sound a little shaky, a little husky, and quite unlike the voice she was more familiar with.

'Of course,' Jack agreed, and pulled her that bit closer, his kiss this time deepening.

Leyne felt all of a tremble inside. She could feel the strength of Jack's body against her own. It was pretty wonderful. 'And…and—and—er—naturally I have to consider…' She drew a shaky breath. Jack might not be kissing her at this moment, but she could still feel the imprint of his body against hers. '…Max. What she would w-want. I mean—'

'Sweetheart,' Jack interrupted her.

She melted at his endearment. 'Yes?'

'Just in case nobody ever told you, there's a time to talk and a time to shut up.'

She stared up at him, loving him with her whole heart. She had no recollection then of how this situation had come about, but to be held in his arms like this, to be kissed by him—she never wanted it to end.

'This—is a time to shut up, right?'

'You're learning fast,' he teased. And wickedly asked, 'With your permission, I'd like to teach you a little more?'

She looked at him. Solemn-eyed, she looked at him. 'I—er—um—think I'm feeling a bit nervous.'

His answer was to kiss her long, lingeringly— and with ever-increasing passion. 'How are you feeling now?' he asked.

Drowning about covered it! 'Fine,' she choked—
and with that one word it appeared she had given
him the permission he had requested to teach her
all he would.

'Little darling,' he breathed, and pulled her closer
to him. He kissed her. She loved him. She kissed
him in return.

He smiled encouragingly, and placed tender
kisses on the corners of her mouth. She smiled at
him and felt all squishy inside. His hands roved her
back. She loved the touch of his hands. She wanted
to explore him too, and with her arms around him
caressed him as he caressed her.

It was wonderful being kissed by him, and, as
passion soared between them, to move over to the
bed seemed only natural.

They were standing next to the bed when she
suddenly became aware that when before he had
been wearing a light sweater, he was now shirt
clad. She hadn't even been aware that he had
removed his sweater. She had to admit it *was*
getting a little hot in here.

She felt his hands at the hem of her lightweight
sweater, and, wearing a shirt beneath, had not the
smallest objection to make when he helped her out
of her sweater.

'All right, Leyne?' he queried gently, as he started
to unfasten the buttons on her shirt.

'Jack, I…I think so,' she answered bravely, and

was unexpectedly taken by a desire to unbutton his shirt. 'Fair's fair,' she whispered, and reached to unfasten one of his buttons.

'How enchanting you are,' he murmured, and with a smile he left unfastening her for a moment to haul her into his arms and hold her fast against him in what to Leyne, at that moment, seemed to be a loving embrace.

What happened after that was purely sensational to her. Leyne had thought they had passionately kissed before, but standing with each other, near na-ked—their shirts discarded—feeling the naked skin of his chest against her, kindled a fire that did not merely spark into life within her but, as his kiss plundered her mouth, demanding a response, posi-tively roared.

She felt his hands at her breasts, and wanted him so badly. He removed her bra and she oddly felt no shame, only joy. This was what she had been waiting for, who she had been waiting for—Jack, her love.

Leyne was not thinking, only feeling when he bent and took part of her swollen breast into his mouth. 'I want you,' she whispered to his bent head.

He heard, raised his head. 'Oh, my darling girl,' he breathed, her desire for him obvious in her eyes. He kissed her and, while kissing her, removed the rest of her clothes. The rest of her clothing that was, with the exception of her briefs, which, in a most peculiar moment of modesty, given the circumstances, Leyne put a hand down to prevent him removing. He was not offended but understanding, even teasing as, 'Two can play that game,' he murmured, and divested himself of all but his one undergarment.

And at last he took her with him to lie down on top of her bed. And it was heaven, pure and simple, to be held, to be caressed, and to have Jack trail kisses over her body.

Her pink-tipped breasts seemed to fascinate him as he kissed and moulded them and tormented their hardened peaks. 'Sweet darling,' he said tenderly in her ear, and came to half lie over her, his hands going to her briefs as if now, if she had no objection to make, he would remove them. 'All right?' he queried.

'Yes,' she answered.

'Shall I make you mine?'

Oh, Jack—Jack, yes. She was in a torment for him. 'Yes,' she answered shyly, but, remembering her manners, 'Please,' she added.

And he laughed. 'You're wonderful!' he cried, and had gently moved her briefs below her hips when suddenly a sound of inner protest—as if he had just remembered something—broke from him. 'No,' he groaned. 'No,' he protested again, and, while staying on the bed with her, he rolled from her, putting some daylight between them.

'What?' she asked. And, sitting up, blushing furiously, 'I was too eager? I've put you off?'

'Oh, Leyne, no, no.' He was sitting up too, facing her, his hands on her shoulders. 'Don't ever think that. You are sweet and adorable with your innocent responses. I'm at fault, not you.'

That admission made her feel a good deal better. 'Well, pardon my naïvety, but I didn't spot it.'

'Adorable, did I say?' He smiled.

'I'm starting to feel a bit awkward, sitting here with next to nothing on,' she confessed. She hitched up her briefs, but after all they had recently shared she saw no sense in prevaricating. 'We're—um— not going to…are we?'

'Dear Leyne,' he murmured softly. 'I never thought…' He broke off, and then openly explained, 'I haven't any protection with me.'

It took a second or two for that to sink in, but when it did, 'It's all right,' she began. 'I haven't been with anyone—' She broke off and went scarlet with embarrassment—it was as if she was *asking* him to make love to her!

She might have scooted off the bed then, but, observing her scarlet cheeks, Jack quickly placed an arm about her shoulders, holding her there. 'I wasn't thinking of *me*,' he stated.

She was more than a mite confused and sought clarification. 'You're saying that you…?'

'No. No, I'm not. You have nothing to fear in that area.' He gave her his word. 'But—and I think I can make a one hundred per cent accurate guess here—

I'd say you're not taking any form of contraception.'
Leyne turned in his arm to stare at him. 'Think
about it, Leyne,' he went on. 'I could make you
pregnant.'

Her mouth fell open. To conceive his child was
something in the heat of the moment she had just
not given thought to. But, now that she had, Leyne
knew that she would very much like to have Jack
Dangerfield's babies.

Only that would never happen—and she felt quite
sad about that thought. Which left her opting for flip-
pancy to hide it. She heaved a dramatic sigh. 'I don't
know, Jack Dangerfield, my one chance to find out
what it's all about—and you go all noble on me!'

He laughed, it was a lovely sound, and she felt all
weak about him again. 'I could possibly arrange for
you to find out at a later date,' he offered, laughter
lurking, for all his expression was now po-faced.

She wanted to laugh, could feel it bubbling up
inside, but managed to be equally po-faced when
she primly answered, 'I don't think so.'

'You don't?'

'This—what happened—was spontaneous
between us.' Her prim note returned. 'I don't really
think I want to make an appointment to lose my
virginity.'

He nodded, as though in full agreement, but soon
brought her uppity primness crumbling when he
smilingly told her, 'I don't know how you can

sound so prim when I know better than most what you've just been up to.'

On cue, she blushed, and he seemed captivated, and just had to haul her into his arms. She did not object. How could she? She wanted to be held by him. He placed his lips over hers, held her close, and at once, as her breasts came into contact with his naked chest, she was again on fire for him.

But he manfully dragged his mouth from hers. 'This has to stop,' he informed her.

'I know,' she said, and kissed him.

Leyne felt his hands on her ribcage as if he was about to push her away. But, after another stifled groan, his hands slid upwards and he captured her breasts in his warm hold.

But too soon he yanked his hands away, pulling back. 'No!' He drew back, removing his hands to look down, his eyes going down to her breasts as though trying to get some message through to his wayward senses.

Leyne leaned into him. They kissed—then abruptly he was pushing her away from him. Yet it seemed as if he was unable to prevent himself from glancing again to her fascinating breasts.

But in the next instant he was off the bed. 'Time for a cold shower,' he said, his voice all thick in his throat, all gravelly as, making for the door, 'Don't you dare come anywhere near me for a good twenty minutes,' he growled.

Leyne smiled when he had gone. Then wanted him back with her. But within five minutes she was starting to wonder how on earth she would ever face him again! Had it not been for that little matter of contraception, he would…she would…

Leyne thought it might be a good idea if she had a shower too, and freshened up. She thought about their lovemaking, thought about him. She did not have to wonder what had come over her that all through her teenage years and into her early twenties she had allowed no man the freedom she had allowed Jack. Plainly and simply, she loved Jack with such a consuming passion she had not had to consider what she was doing—it had just seemed—so right.

She felt calmer once she was dressed, but, while she still had an overwhelming need to see Jack, her love, she was in no hurry to join him downstairs. While loving him meant that making love with him had seemed natural, she felt awkward now that she was back in a world where she had space to think.

She had been eager for his kisses; she knew that she had been. He knew it too. But had he discerned that at the root of her eagerness had been her love for him? She would just die if he had. Though perhaps all his women-friends behaved in that fashion?

Leyne did not care very much for that last thought, and went over to the window seat, wishing that John Dangerfield and Pip would soon return.

Pip would have eaten, so she need not think about food for her. Though, as she all at once experienced a feeling of reluctance to go downstairs, where it would be just her and Jack, Leyne decided that for herself she could do without lunch.

Which was why a half an hour later she was still in her room when Jack Dangerfield came knocking at her door. Since there were only two of them in the house, it had to be him.

Feeling all flustered suddenly, Leyne knew she would have to go and answer it. She felt all churned up inside as she went over to the door and pulled it back.

Jack stood there, relaxed, easy, with no problem whatsoever to see her. She went red. She had known that she would. 'You knocked!' she exclaimed in mock surprise.

He ignored her sarcasm, not a scrap wounded by it, his glance kind as he observed her blush. She loved him. 'I think it better I don't enter your room,' he remarked, and, as Leyne followed through that remark, she realised he could only be referring to what had happened the last time he had walked in unannounced. Surely he wasn't saying that he didn't trust himself...?

'I—er...' She was stumped.

But not so he. 'I've made us some lunch. I thought you might be feeling a little reticent about joining me.'

There had been no sign of reticence about her not so long ago, she recalled, feeling pink about her cheeks again. 'You know too much about women!' she informed him waspishly.

'It's an art,' he admitted. And, soon putting paid to her waspishness, 'Please may I have my clothes back?' he asked nicely.

She folded. She had to laugh. She did not want to, but couldn't help it. He just did that to her. Without a word she turned and collected the neat bundle she had made of his belongings and took them over to him.

He took them from her. 'Come on, Leyne,' he said seriously.

'I'll be down in a minute,' she promised. He took her at her word and left her to join him in her own time.

Any awkwardness she might have felt when a short while later she joined him in the kitchen was soon done away with as Jack took the conversation into other areas. He asked about her work—did she enjoy it, how long had she been doing it, and had she ever considered doing anything else?

'Not really,' she replied to his last question. 'I enjoy what I'm doing.'

'Still seeing the boyfriend?'

'Keith?' she asked, and grinned as she explained, 'I don't think I'm top of his hit parade any more.'

'The man has no stamina!' Jack scorned.

But Leyne did not want to discuss Keith Collins. She wanted to know more about the man sitting opposite her. 'How about you?'

'What about me? Am I still seeing the girlfriend?'

'I'm not interested in your love-life!' Liar! Darts of evil green battered her. 'Do you enjoy the work you do? And how long have you been chairman?'

'I wouldn't want to do anything else,' Jack replied, going on, 'When, a few years ago, my father decided I was up to taking over from him, he retired.' But, plainly a man who did not like talking about himself, he switched the conversation to enquire, 'I take it Maxine hasn't been in touch?'

Leyne revealed how it had been Ben Turnbull who had been in touch, and that her sister must have been very seriously ill. 'According to him, Max is making a good recovery, but I shall feel happier when I've spoken to her personally. Ben Turnbull has said she will ring me some time next week.'

'You'll have a lot to discuss.'

Leyne did not need any reminding, and, their meal finished, she began clearing away, hoping again that she had done the right thing and that Max would not be upset.

She decided to wash the dishes by hand, and was surprised when Jack came and picked up the drying-up cloth. She guessed her look must have said as much, because he good-humouredly informed her, 'You're the guest here. If I was any sort of a host I would insist you put your feet up the whole weekend.'

Which unfortunately brought to her mind the fact that she had done that very thing—on her bed— with him. She realised he must have followed her thoughts when he quirked an eyebrow. But just then they heard the sound of a car and, her attention taken up with thoughts of Pip, Leyne left the kitchen.

She found that Jack was right beside her, and it was he who went forwards and opened the door to his father and one very happy young girl.

'Have a good time, poppet?' he asked her.

'Great!' she answered, and went past him to where Leyne was standing.

'You got everything you needed?' Leyne asked, eyeing the carrier with its art shop logo that she was holding.

'Everything!' Pip answered enthusiastically. 'Shall I take it upstairs?'

Leyne stifled the impulse to go with her. She wanted to know how her morning had gone, but did not want the other two to think she was about to give her the third degree over it.

'That's a good idea,' she said instead. 'You can leave your coat while you're up there.' And, while Pip went cheerfully on her way, 'Have you had coffee?' Leyne asked John Dangerfield, and was instantly embarrassed that, as Jack had said, she was a guest here, he the host.

But, before she could apologise, Jack was politely requesting, 'May I have one too?'

He really was super, Leyne couldn't help thinking as she made a pot of adult coffee for three and a milky cup for Pip. It had crossed her mind that father and son might want some time to talk in private, and that she and Pip should disappear and make themselves scarce. Against that, though, John Dangerfield's prime aim in coming here today had been to become acquainted with his daughter. Perhaps she and Pip would drink their coffee and then disappear. Leyne decided to see how it went.

Pip came and found her in the kitchen, and seemed to be feeling very grown-up to have been out to lunch with Mr Dangerfield. Leyne sorely wanted to ask what they had talked about, but something within her would not let her. Besides, she knew from experience that over the course of the next few days and weeks, in a dribbled sentence here and there, she would hear from Pip all that there was to hear. And, for the moment, the fact that Pip had enjoyed her outing and had returned happy and well adjusted was sufficient.

Her niece helped her carry the trays with coffee and china into the drawing room, where Jack pulled forward a long low table in front of a sofa. While Leyne poured coffee, Pip took the first cup and saucer over to the gentleman she had lunched with.

But when everyone had their coffee Leyne found

herself sitting on the sofa next to Jack, while Pip was sitting on a small padded chair near to John Dangerfield.

Conversation, following on from the fact that Pip and the man who was her father had found time to browse in a bookshop that morning too, was about books, and what Pip was currently reading. But all of a sudden Leyne spotted that her niece was staring hard and thoughtfully at him. And also that she had got that well-known direct look in her forthright green eyes.

Pip's gaze was concentrated solely on him, and she was looking at no one but the man who, with the exception of the wings of white at his temples, had the same jet hair as she had, and the same green eyes. Leyne suddenly realised too that she was not the only one who had noticed Pip's intent gaze, because all at once, as John Dangerfield became aware of that highly concentrated direct gaze on him, all conversation abruptly ceased.

And his gaze was equally direct while he waited quietly for her to form what she wanted to say. On Leyne's part, she had no clue to what was going through Pip's mind. That was until suddenly, in a very clear voice, the eleven-and-a-half-year-old stated, 'My mother is a photographer.'

Startled, Leyne was at once ready to intercede, and made to leave the sofa. But, before she could move or say a word, she was further startled when

Jack, who had obviously recalled Pip saying the self-same thing to him, caught a hold of her arm, anchoring her there. Leyne might well have attempted to shrug off his grip had she not just then remembered Jack's promise that his father would not hurt Pip, and would say nothing to upset her.

'So I understand,' John Dangerfield responded, green eyes holding green eyes.

'Her name is Maxine Nicholson,' Pip told him solemnly, a look of intense single-mindedness on her sweet features. He said nothing. And then, Leyne expecting it, but not ready for it, 'Do you know her?' Pip asked.

Panicking, Leyne made a small involuntary movement, but Jack's hold was firm, making her still when his father replied, 'Yes, Pip, I know your mother.'

Pip's mouth formed a rounded 'O' but no sound came. But, after a huge breath, her eyes focussed solely on him. 'Are you...?' she began, faltered, and then, with a determination Leyne knew from experience little would budge, she stayed in there to ask in a rush, 'Are you my father?'

The whole room seemed to be holding its breath as it waited for his answer. All Leyne's protective instincts were rampant, but—and she recognised it enough to sit still—Pip had waited a long, long while for this. Without knowing it Leyne had somehow caught a hold of Jack's hand.

She was holding it tightly when, looking nowhere but into his daughter's waiting green eyes, 'Yes, Pip, I am,' John Dangerfield told her. And he smiled at her then, as he asked, 'Do you mind that?'

Leyne watched spellbound as Pip continued to stare at him. And then, as politely as she could, 'You're a bit older than I imagined,' she said plainly. 'But I think you are very nice.'

She turned from him then, and looked over to Leyne, and then left her chair to come over to her. Leyne could see that Pip was a little flushed, but her breathing was even, no sign of a cough, and apart from that flush of colour she was otherwise all right.

'Did you know that Mr Dangerfield was my father?' Pip asked her.

'Leyne found out last night,' Jack filled in for her. And discovered that he was the object of Pip's steady green-eyed scrutiny.

Once more green eyes fixed on green eyes, then Pip was telling him, 'I thought it was you at first.' She was still giving him that direct Dangerfield look when, with a smile trying to break through, she brought out that which her young intelligence had suddenly brought her. 'I suppose…' she thought it through '…that if Mr Dangerfield is my dad, and if he is your dad too, you—must be my brother!' And, with the most wonderful grin, 'Do *you* mind that?' she asked.

Jack's answer was to fix his green eyes on her

green eyes. 'I should be honoured to have you for a sister,' he declared.

Pip grinned with him for a few brilliantly happy seconds, before she turned to study the man who had just stated that he was her father. 'Will I do?' he asked, when endless seconds had ticked by without her saying a word.

Her reply was to give him a wonderful beaming smile. 'Yes,' she answered simply. And suddenly became shy. Leyne, in her role as loving aunt first, trusted guardian second, took over.

'Shall we take the coffee cups out to the kitchen?' she suggested—and only then did Leyne become aware that she had been gripping on to Jack's hand with enough force to fracture it. 'Sorry,' she mumbled as she got to her feet and, with Pip's help, began to restack the trays.

'Think nothing of it,' he murmured, easing his fingers. 'What are boyfriends for?'

Leyne did not answer. If only! But there were other more important issues here than to wish for the moon.

CHAPTER EIGHT

LEYNE owned to feeling quite drained when Jack dropped them back at their home on Sunday. Somehow she could not be natural with him. She full well knew why that was, of course. She was in love with him, and, while there was every chance he had caught a glimpse of her feelings for him—and while she desperately hoped that he had not—pride demanded that she show him he was entirely mistaken.

Not that he seemed one whit bothered. While being quite pleasant, Leyne felt that there was an aloof edge to his pleasantness. Well, he needn't bother being aloof. She might be a little on the in-experienced side—well, quite a lot, actually—when playing in his league, but she could read the signs. Jack Dangerfield clearly regretted their lovemaking interlude and was trying to put across that it would not happen again—i.e. that there was no future for them short term, and very definitely not long term.

'Goodbye, Jack!' Pip chirruped as he toted their weekend bags to the door.

'Bye, poppet,' he said, and bent to give her a kiss.

No way! Leyne kept well out of pecking shot when he straightened. She need not have concerned herself. 'Bye, Leyne,' he said crisply, and she could tell he had never been going to kiss her, with or without the signals he so obviously had picked up.

For all her bravado, Leyne felt close to tears once she had the door closed and heard him drive away. Pip asking one of her direct questions momentarily diverted her, for all the question was in regard to him.

'Have you and Jack fallen out?' she asked, and Leyne was again reminded of how perceptive her little niece was proving to be.

'No, of course not!' Leyne forced a light laugh. 'But we were never very serious about each other.'

'You met him when you were looking for my father?'

'I did,' Leyne replied, watching her closely, as she had since yesterday afternoon, for any sign of trauma. There was none.

Indeed, Pip had never seemed more content now that she knew, and had met, the man who was her father. 'Thank you for finding him for me, Leyne,' she said sweetly. 'My dad.'

'Oh, darling!' Leyne exclaimed, and caught her close and gave her a hug. 'Now,' she said, 'we'd better go and check what you need for school tomorrow.'

Over the next few days Leyne jumped every time the telephone rang. It was never Jack. She knew it would not be, but still the same could do nothing to stop the feeling of disappointment that it was not.

Which, she freely owned, was quite ridiculous. Why would he ring her? She doubted she would ever see him again, let alone speak to him. Mystery solved, duty done—farewell, Leyne Rowberry!

Her mother had telephoned from her holiday hotel on Monday, and Leyne had not known where to begin to tell her half of what had taken place since they had last been in contact. But, having been told that Leyne and Pip had met John Danger-field, and that Ben Turnbull had rung and why, her mother was more concerned that Maxine had been ill, and Leyne had spent most of the phone call assuring her that Max was making a good recovery.

'You'd better tell her to give me a ring when she calls,' Catherine Webb had instructed.

'I will,' Leyne had promised, and had taken down the hotel's phone number and her mother's room number.

The call Leyne had been anticipating from her sister came through on Wednesday, early evening. Pip would normally have been there, but that evening she was at her friend Alice's house, working on a team project.

Leyne was overjoyed to hear Max at last—and a Max who was sounding all bright and bubbly. After explaining Pip's absence, and saying how sorry Pip would be to have missed her, 'How are you, Max?' Leyne asked.

'Couldn't be better,' Max replied. 'Ben said he'd told you what had happened.'

'You're sure you're fully recovered? You're not just saying that—?'

'I'm fine, honestly,' Max interrupted. 'It was a bit—er—not too good for a while…'

'You were *delirious*!' Leyne exclaimed.

'Well, I'm not now—um—other than with happiness!'

'What? You—?'

'Ben,' Max cut in, and, unable to hold it down any longer, 'He's asked me to marry him!'

'Marry…!' Leyne gasped. 'I didn't think you liked him all that well!'

'I didn't—to start with. At the beginning I could have as easily hit him as speak to him. But…' her voice softened '…then I got ill—and he was little short of wonderful. He looked after me night and day…'

'Oh, Maxie,' Leyne said softly. Clearly, as she had surmised, her sister had been very ill. 'You said yes? To his marriage proposal?'

'I said yes,' Max agreed. 'As I got well again, I started to see a different side of him, a caring side I never suspected existed. I just—fell in love with him—and he with me.'

'I'm so glad for you,' Leyne said. Max's news was something of a bombshell. Leyne had a bombshell of her own to drop, but hesitated to spoil her sister's mood of utter happiness by telling her all that had happened this side of the world.

'Will—um—you be marrying before you come home?' she prevaricated for a small while, knowing that any minute now she was going to have to tell her.

'We're coming home early,' Max announced. 'All being well, we'll be home for Christmas. We'll probably get married some time in January—Ben can't see any reason to wait. You, along with Pip, will be my bridesmaid, of course.'

'Of course,' Leyne agreed.

'And naturally I shall want Pip and you to move into Ben's place with me when I go.'

'Oh, I don't know about that, Max. Ben will want—'

'He has a large house, and he says there will be plenty of room. It will probably mean you leaving your present job, and Pip will definitely have to move to another school. But we'll discuss all of that when we get home.'

It was more than a bit of a shock that Pip would be going to live somewhere else, and Max too, though Leyne wanted above all that they be happy. But she needed time to think if she wanted to leave her job and move with them.

'As you say, we'll discuss it when you get home,'

she said, not wanting to put a damper on her sister's elated mood by putting up barriers.

'Meantime,' Max went on, 'I have to confess I'm a wee bit anxious about how Pip will take all of this.'

'How do you mean?' Leyne asked. Pip was always a most compliant child—well, nearly always.

'After all these years of living in a male-free home, how do you think she'll react to Ben? Do you think she'll take to having him for a father?'

'Er...' Leyne murmured, and knew that she could delay no longer. The time had come to tell Max everything, and to hope she would understand. 'The thing is...' she began, the words sticking in her throat.

'What?' Max asked urgently. 'What's happened? What's wrong?'

'Nothing's wrong,' Leyne quickly assured her. 'It's just that—well, to tell you the truth, your plane had barely taken off for places foreign when Pip asked me if I knew who her father was.' Leyne halted at Max's audible gasp of shock.

'I was going to tell her, but I kept putting it off!' she exclaimed. 'Has she asked again since?'

'She needed to know, Max. She'd got that direct look about her.'

'I know the one.'

'Anyway, when it was clear that it wasn't just a whim, and that it had been on Pip's mind for some while, I went to see Mother.'

'She told you Pip's father is a man named John

Dangerfield,' Max guessed, and, swiftly taking on board what she must do, 'I'd better contact him,' she stated.

'In—um—a roundabout way—I already have.'

'You have?'

'It wouldn't wait.'

'Oh, Leyne, I'm sorry. You couldn't contact me and—' she broke off. 'Does Pip know?' she asked, concerned.

'She knows,' Leyne confirmed, and had to add, 'She's met him.'

'She's *met* him?'

'Please don't worry, Max. He was really lovely with her.'

'He would be. He's a very special kind of man.' Max was silent for a moment, then confessed, 'I never thought I would ever fall in love again after John, but…' Her voice faded, and Leyne guessed Max's thoughts were on her future husband.

'You're not angry with me?' Leyne asked.

'Of course I'm not!' Max straight away exclaimed. 'You were put in a dreadful position. But I'd better have a chat to Pip ASAP. I'll ring again before her bedtime.'

'She'd love that,' Leyne replied. 'Oh, and can you ring Mother, too? I told her you had been ill, but were recovering well, but she won't believe it until she hears it from you yourself. She and Roland are on holiday. If you've got a pen I'll give you their number.'

By the time their call had ended, Max had recovered from her shock about Pip wanting to know who her father was, and was talking Ben again. 'I'll call again in an hour or so,' she said as she rang off.

When Leyne went to collect Pip she decided against telling her that her mother would be calling her that night. Apart from anything else, Pip would be sorely disappointed should some technical hitch or hold-up prevent Max from getting through.

She and Pip had been home for about only fifteen minutes and were in the kitchen when the phone rang. 'Would you like to get that?' Leyne asked, with an inner smile as she anticipated her niece's delight.

But no sooner had Pip gone than, her face beaming, she was rushing back again. 'My brother's on the phone!' she announced proudly—and Leyne, fully expecting it to be Max, just wasn't with her.

'Your brother?'

'Jack!' Pip grinned. 'He wants a word.'

'Ah!' Leyne exclaimed, her heart racing suddenly. Hoping she had not gone red, Leyne went to the phone. 'Hello,' she said.

'How's Pip?' he asked without preamble, making it plain to Leyne, lest she should imagine he had any interest at all in calling for any reason other than his new-found little sister, that his call was about Pip.

Bully for him, Leyne thought, ready to straight away let him know that she would not want him to

call for any other reason. 'Very happy,' she answered coolly.

'There haven't been any repercussions?'

'None at all,' she replied woodenly.

'Hmph. Good,' he grunted, but stayed on the line
to enquire, 'Any new men in your life?'

Leyne had no idea what had brought about that
sort of a question, but she very much hoped it was
not from any notion that she might be pining for him.
'What can I tell you? I work for a firm full of them.'

'Never a week goes by, huh?'

'You must experience something similar,' she
commented off-handedly, jealousy darts aiming
their spiteful spears.

'All the time,' he answered.

'Enjoy,' she wished him.

Leyne felt unsettled after his call, though owned
that she had not felt all that settled *before* he had rung.
But almost immediately the phone rang again. Leyne
left Pip to answer it. This time it *was* Max, and Leyne
waited in the kitchen for Pip to come and find her.

What seemed like an age later, Pip came bursting
into the kitchen. 'That was my mum!' she exclaimed breathlessly. 'She told me all about my
father and how they met and… and…my mum's
going to marry Ben Turnbull—and we're going to
be bridesmaids. And she'll be home for Christmas—all being well!'

Pip was on such a high after her phone call that

Leyne let her stay up for an extra half an hour. Only when her niece was in bed, however, did Leyne have a chance to sort out her thoughts and feelings that had been up, down and jumbled—starting first of all with the phone call from Max, and becoming more down than up following that phone call from Jack.

While it pleased her that he had given thought to how Pip might be faring since she had learned the identity of her father, Leyne half wished that he had not phoned. She did not wish to think of him 'all the time' enjoying success with his female companions.

As for her other phone call, she could not have been more pleased that Max had found happiness with Ben Turnbull. But, while knowing that she would miss her sister when she moved to Ben Turnbull's home, and would miss Pip quite dreadfully, Leyne thought that would be a selfish reason to move in with them. Somehow she was going to have to find the strength to make the break. It was just not on that Max should start her married life with her sister in tow.

Having established that, Leyne gave thought to what she might do to fill the void of not thinking first of Pip in all that she did. It was not something she looked forward to. The little love had entered her heart on day one, and with her growing years that strength of feeling for her niece had grown and cemented. Leyne knew she would miss her like crazy.

Leyne considered that she would quite like to

have a baby to lavish her love on. But the only father she could imagine for her child was Jack Dangerfield—and that was just not going to happen.

He would take jolly good care of that! He had shown very clearly that, while he might well enjoy a brief bedroom interlude with her, he had soon come to his senses on realising he could very well make her pregnant.

It seemed to her then that Jack had backed away fast ever since then. She blushed anew at the thought that he must have seen her love for him.

Which was why when, on answering the phone on Friday evening, and discovering much to her surprise that it was none other than the man who seemed to possess most of her waking thoughts, she was at pains to show him just how wrong he was if he thought she cared one iota for him.

'How's Pip?' he asked.

'She's fine,' Leyne responded, it being a foregone conclusion that he had not phoned to enquire after *her* health.

'No problems?'

Leyne did not care for his nerve. They had nurtured Pip for going on twelve years. Any problems they would solve, as they always had. 'There's no need for you to be concerned,' she answered coolly.

'Or ring every five minutes?'

'Pardon?'

'Isn't that what you're telling me?'

Jack had obviously picked up from her tone that she did not regard him as her best friend. Good! 'Are you looking for a fight?' she challenged snappily. She'd die if he glimpsed so much as a hint of how wobbly she felt inside just from speaking to him.

A long pause followed her challenge, so that for a moment Leyne thought he had ended his call. Then, as if making an effort, 'Shall we start again?' he enquired mildly.

Leyne got it then. Quite plainly, having met his new sister, and already having some regard for Pip and towards her welfare, he, in the interests of family harmony, was swallowing any 'get lost' annoyance he was feeling with one Leyne Rowberry.

She was about to take the battle to him when Leyne suddenly saw that she would not be acting in Max's best interests to antagonise the other half of Pip's kin. 'So,' she said, fighting a battle to stay aloof so he should not have any confirmation of her feelings for him, while at the same time realising that she had to bend a little, 'how are you?'

'As well as can be expected,' he replied, and she could have sworn she could hear a smile in his voice at her more yielding tone. 'Actually, I was wondering what you were doing tomorrow evening?'

For one glorious second Leyne thought he was asking her out. Reality slammed in. As if! 'You're offering to sit with Pip while I go out?' she enquired, striving to sound friendly.

'You've a date tomorrow?' he rapped.

With a basket of ironing, actually. 'If I can get a sitter,' she lied. She'd had the offer of dinner on Saturday, but had turned it down. 'How are you fixed?' she asked, certain in advance that he would have better things planned than to babysit his young sister.

As was proved correct when, 'I'm busy!' he retorted. Phone down, end of conversation.

Leyne was sure she did not care who he was seeing that kept him 'busy'. But she did, and she hated him—momentarily—that it should hurt so.

Come Saturday morning, however, and Dianne Gardner phoned to say that Alice would not be able to go swimming that morning. She had only just informed her mother that she had lost her trainers.

'How can anyone lose their trainers, I ask you? She had them for Games yesterday morning!' Dianne complained. 'Anyhow, the upshot is that if Alice wants trainers for Games next week, this morning is the only chance I have of taking her into town to get some new ones.' Dianne paused, and then asked, 'Would Pip want to come with us?'

'Are you sure?'

'It will probably be better if Pip's there—she seems to have more sense than Alice.'

'Just a moment. I'll ask her,' Leyne said, and

turned to Pip, who was hovering, and whom Leyne suspected had known all about the lost trainers. 'Swimming or shopping?'

'Tough decision,' Pip answered with a grin. 'But I think I'll take shopping.'

An hour later, having just said goodbye to Dianne and the two girls, Leyne realised she might be able to fit some ironing into her amended morning timetable. She had just finished tidying up, however, when the doorbell sounded and, on going to answer it, Leyne was very much surprised to see Pip's father standing there.

'I hope I haven't called at an inconvenient moment?' John Dangerfield said apologetically. And, explaining the book in his hand, 'I was in a bookshop yesterday and remembered Pip likes Jacqueline Wilson. Has she read this one? I'm told it's her latest.'

Leyne wasn't very sure what she was supposed to do in a situation like this—Pip's father calling out of the blue. But John Dangerfield was also the father of the man she loved, and that alone entitled him to visiting rights.

'I don't think she has—she's out shopping with a friend and her friend's mother at the moment. But—would you like to come in?'

Apparently he would. Leyne invited him into the sitting room and slipped out to make some coffee. She joined him shortly afterwards and discovered that she felt quite comfortable, sitting drinking coffee with Jack's father.

'I wasn't certain you would be in,' he commented easily. 'Jack mentioned that you take Pip and her friend swimming most Saturday mornings.'

'Shopping was a bigger attraction this morning.'

He smiled at that, and sensitively remarked, 'Jack tells me you're fiercely independent. But you would tell me if there is anything my daughter needs?'

'I don't think—'

'Indulge me, Leyne,' he requested seriously. 'I've neglected her for far too long.'

'You didn't even know you had a daughter until just over a week ago,' she excused him.

'True,' he agreed. 'But now that I do know, I cannot possibly leave it at that.'

Leyne stared at him, this handsome sixty-year-old. 'I'm not sure I understand what you mean?' she queried slowly. 'We've seen to it that Pip wants for nothing. We—'

'It isn't only things financial,' he cut in to explain. 'From what I can gather, you had no idea who Pip's father was before you began making enquiries. And while it grieves me that Maxine kept my daughter's existence from me, I should, for a start, like to have Pip re-registered, showing me as her father on her birth certificate.'

As Jack had said, his father was an honourable man, but Leyne was not the one he should be talking to. 'You'd have to discuss that with Max,' she replied, knowing that would have to be Max's choice, not hers. There would also be Ben Turnbull to consider—he might well want to adopt Pip. It was all starting to get a little complicated.

'I'd also like to spend some time with Pip. Start getting to know her, let her get to know her father. I'd like—'

'Oh, I don't know about that, Mr Dangerfield,' Leyne interrupted quickly.

'John, please,' he invited. And, unaffronted, 'Something about my getting to know my daughter bothers you?'

'It isn't that. And, speaking for myself, I feel sure Pip would like to get to know you too. But there are other factors involved here.'

'None, I feel certain, we cannot come to an agreement over. Is there anything in particular that might worry you and Maxine?' he enquired pleasantly.

'Well—we wouldn't want to do anything—er—underhand,' Leyne plunged.

'Underhand?' He seemed a touch taken aback.

'Your wife...' Leyne began.

'Oh, yes.' John Dangerfield smiled as he comprehended. 'I appreciate your sentiments, and I endorse them. But you need not worry, Leyne. I intend there to be nothing underhand, hole-and-corner, and I certainly don't intend to keep it dark about my daughter.'

'You don't?'

'I do not,' he answered firmly, and continued, 'While, for Pip's sake, I have no intention of shouting her existence from the rooftops, I equally have no intention of denying her existence. As and when the occasion arises, I shall introduce her as my daughter.'

'The press may get hold of it.'

'I realise that, and I shall guard her. But I had already decided that I must tell my wife everything there was to tell.'

'You're going to tell her?' Leyne exclaimed, startled.

'I already have—last night.'

'Oh, heavens!' Leyne gasped. All they had wanted was for Pip to know the name of her father—and, yes, perhaps to meet him. But this—it was growing out of all proportion, growing out of hand! 'Was she very upset, very shocked?'

'Helen, my wife, was the one who shocked me,' he replied, a fond expression on his face as he recalled how it had been. 'I think Jack may have mentioned something of his mother's horse riding accident? It was a particularly horrendous time for all of us—though more so for her. Anyhow, I had barely got started on telling her the blunt truth that when she was at her lowest ebb I'd had a—I won't call it an affair—that demeans its sweetness. It was more a romantic interlude. However, before I could tell her about Pip, Helen told me that she knew something had gone on around that time.'

'She'd guessed?'

'She had insisted on a divorce and refused to see me. Which rather floored me, I admit. But when I picked myself up, got myself back together, and decided I was going to fight for what was mine, I let her know that I wasn't having any of that divorce nonsense. From then on I spent hours just sitting with her. But she's a very intuitive woman, my Helen, and apparently there were so many times when I couldn't meet her eyes that she just knew something had happened. She let me off lightly,' he commented, 'and said it was a relief to know at last—and to know it was long over.'

'You—told her about Pip?'

He nodded. 'Helen has agreed that I need to have a hand in my child's upbringing and welfare.'

'Oh, I'm not certain Max would—'

'Don't upset yourself,' he butted in quickly. 'I'll sort something amicable out with Maxine. I can fly out to where she is, if need be—'

'Max rang last night,' Leyne interrupted. 'She is cutting short her trip and hopes to be home in time for Christmas.'

'Splendid! Christmas is only weeks away.'

'Max has just got engaged,' Leyne confided. 'She's planning to be married in January.'

'I'm glad,' John Dangerfield said with a smile.

'She is such a lovely person, and she deserves a
world of happiness.' And, coffee finished, their chat
at an end, he got to his feet. 'I promise you, Leyne,
that I have not the slightest intention of doing
anything that might put a blight on her happiness.'

Leyne remembered that when he had gone.
Whenever she thought of him wanting a hand in his
daughter's upbringing and welfare, and started to
worry that what he wanted might not be what Max
would want, she would remember how he had said
he had no intention of doing anything that might put
a blight on her sister's happiness. Added to that,
Leyne recalled Max saying that John Dangerfield
was a very special kind of man, and Leyne somehow
had a feeling that, as he had said, he and Max would
be able to amicably sort something out about Pip.

Well before Pip arrived home, John Dangerfield's son was back in residence in Leyne's head
again. Jack was very taken with Pip too, Leyne
knew, so felt it would be no surprise if he too
wanted to have some input when it came to deci-
sions about his little sister.

Perhaps, Leyne mused, they would meet, she
and Jack. Hope stirred—she flattened it. This was
no way to live, hoping to see him yet having to
watch every word in case she slipped up somehow
and gave away something of her feelings for him.

Leyne was glad when Dianne dropped Pip off.
'Enjoy your morning?' she asked her.

224 PROMISE OF A FAMILY

'It was great!'

'Alice managed to get her trainers?'

'Not the ones she wanted,' Pip replied. 'But she gave in when Mrs Gardner said it was the ones she'd selected or nothing.'

'You had a visitor while you were out,' Leyne smilingly told her.

'Who?' Pip asked, her eyes going wide.

'The same man who took you shopping last Saturday,' Leyne said, and, handing her the book, 'He brought this for you.'

'Oh, Leyne,' Pip whispered, taking the book from her and turning it over in her hands. 'Fancy him remembering I like—' She broke off as she opened the book and examined the fly-leaf—something Leyne had not thought to do, 'Oh, Leyne!' she whispered again, and suddenly her eyes were brimming with tears.

Leyne took the book from her. '"To Pip".' She read what he had written. '"From her father, John Dangerfield".' Leyne handed the book back to her and had to turn away—her eyes were suddenly brimming too.

A hug and a short while later they were both back to normal, and, though disappointed at having missed seeing her father, Leyne noticed that Pip seemed to be carrying her book around with her from room to room. Leyne felt then that she had been right to do what she had. To know her father was clearly of the utmost importance to her little niece.

Pip was her normal cheerful self by the time she went up to bed that evening. Leyne contemplated going to bed herself, but on checking the clock she decided it was a little early. Besides which, for all she had recently started to have trouble sleeping, she was not in the least tired.

She knew whose fault that was, though—and Jack Dangerfield was in her head again. Was this how it was going to be? she wondered. Her evenings, her free time, stretching out before her while she waited for it to get better? While she waited to get over Mr Jack Dangerfield?

Leyne tried to pin her thoughts on other matters. She should start to look forward to Christmas. For Pip's sake she would make an effort. Max would be home soon and…Leyne couldn't keep it up. Jack was back. And all at once it hit her full square that— even though she had thought she had flattened hope—she must still be hopeful of seeing Jack again.

Fate gave a hollow laugh. What hope had she got of ever seeing him again? When Pip moved out to go and live with her mother and stepfather, there would be absolutely no reason on earth for him to come ringing at this doorbell.

When, just at that exact moment, the front doorbell *did* ring, Leyne nearly jumped out of her skin. She checked her watch. It was half past ten! Who on earth…? Leyne went to answer the door, wondering who in the world came calling at this time of night—at the same time knowing she was going to have to come to terms with the fact that she had seen Jack for the last time—and why, anyway, would she imagine he would want to see her?

A mere diversion to keep his batteries charged—that was all their lovemaking had been to him, she fretted as she pulled open the front door. Then her mind went totally blank for several seconds, because who should be standing there but none other than the man she had only just unhappily realised would never coming ringing at her doorbell again?

Speechlessly she stared at him. 'Good evening,' he said politely.

She opened her mouth, no sound came. 'Er—Pip's in bed,' she managed after a moment.

'At this time of night, I should hope so,' he responded.

'Well—um…' Leyne faltered—she did not want to invite him in. Jack Dangerfield was devastating enough on the doorstep, without having him in the confines of her sitting room. 'I would prefer not to wake her.' She managed to find a cool note.

His eyes narrowed slightly, her cool tone not lost on him. 'I too would prefer that you didn't,' he returned evenly. And, taking a step forward, causing her to take a step back, 'It isn't Pip I'm here to see.'

'Oh,' Leyne murmured, and didn't know what else to say.

Then, as her stunned feelings from seeing him

there so unexpectedly began to adjust, so her thinking power came back. It wasn't Pip he was here to see! Well, Leyne did not kid herself that it was her—*her*—he wanted to see. Jack Dangerfield might not have come to see Pip, but oh so very obviously he had come for some reason connected with Pip.

And, since they both had her niece's interests at heart, 'You'd better come in,' she invited, when at the start she'd had no such intention.

She stood back from the door, but only then, as Jack crossed over the threshold, did she notice that he seemed to have a very determined kind of look in his eyes. It was almost as if he had come here braced—to do battle!

CHAPTER NINE

'So?' LEYNE enquired coolly once they were in the sitting room. Whatever battle he had in mind, for Pip's sake she would be up to it.

Jack looked speculatively back at her. 'Shall we sit down?' he suggested.

She did not thank him for reminding her of her manners. 'The reason for your call is going to take that long?'

Again he studied her, but that determined light in his eyes had in no way diminished. 'By the look of it—very probably,' he answered, and then proceeded to rattle her defences by asking, 'Why are you so antagonistic towards me?'

Oh, heavens! Talk about taking the battle into her camp! 'I'm…' Not, she had been about to say. But that was too obviously a blatant lie. She pulled herself together. 'Would you like to take a seat?' she invited instead.

His lips twitched. 'You're something else again,

Leyne Rowberry,' he murmured as, moving over to an easy chair, he waited until she was first seated opposite before he sat down.

Quite unexpectedly, treacherously, when she was intent on showing him a cool front, she began to feel all warm about him. And all at once it started to feel so good to have him here—even if his visit was on Pip's account and not hers—that Leyne almost offered to make him coffee. Just in time, she came to her senses. Despite the fact that he was now seated, she was still convinced that his business in calling would not take more than a few minutes.

'So?' she said again, but the cool touch of hostility was sadly absent this time.

He ignored her question. 'I thought you had a date tonight?'

'My sitter let me down.'

'Hah!' he exclaimed.

'What—hah?' He didn't believe her—didn't believe she'd had a date. She knew that he didn't.

'That has to be a lie!' He confirmed it.

'No, it isn't!' she denied, refusing to blush. He couldn't know for certain—even if she *was* still lying.

He gave her a sceptical look, 'You, Miss Rowberry,' he stated, 'take your responsibilities for Pip much too seriously to so much as consider leaving her in charge of anyone who might let you down.'

He'd got her there, damn him. 'So?' She brazened it out.

'I don't doubt that there are many men rejected by the wayside,' he commented. But that direct look she knew so well was suddenly there in his eyes. 'Just what does one have to do to get a date with you?' he demanded.

Like he wanted a date with her! 'I thought you were busy tonight?' she countered.

His look said he had not forgotten that he had asked her a question. But he let it go, and, his eyes holding hers, very deliberately he informed her, 'I decided I would rather come and see you.'

'Ah!' she mumbled, looking for breathing space—that had sounded so intimate somehow. 'I—um—think that—er—anything to do with Pip is best discussed between Max and your father,' she threw in. Whatever Jack had come to see her about was, without question, about Pip.

'This isn't—' he began, but Leyne was feeling all soft about him again, and was at pains to hide it.

'Your father popped in this morning, by the way,' she forestalled him. 'Though you probably knew that?'

'I didn't, actually.'

'You've been in touch with neither of your parents recently?'

Jack gave her one of those speculative looks. 'What do you know that I don't?' he strayed from his set course to ask.

Her sensitivities to his mother, and for all his

mother had shaken his father, she must have
received something of a shock herself, caused
Leyne to feel a little awkward. She had no wish for
Jack to be to upset on his mother's behalf.

'Jack—your mother knows,' Leyne said gently.

'About Pip? About my father's infidelity?' he
asked sharply.

Leyne nodded. 'Your father told her.'

'Oh, Lord!' he exclaimed. But, getting himself
back together, 'How did she take it? Has she
demanded a divorce? Has—?'

'Nothing like that,' Leyne replied quickly, and
explained, 'You know all about the terrible—er—
marital time they went through while you were in
Australia? Well, apparently your mother guessed
that something had gone on when too many times
your father couldn't meet her eyes.'

'Hmph. And she was all right about it—when
he told her?'

'I believe it came as something of a relief to her
to know what had happened. She has agreed,
anyhow, that your father needs to be involved with
regard to Pip's wellbeing.'

Jack drew a relieved breath. 'Thank God for
that,' he commented, and confided, 'My mother
was of quite some concern to me when, with
evidence of that DNA, I had to start thinking the
unthinkable.'

'That your father was Pip's father?'

'Exactly. While I have female cousins, the male bloodline stops with me.'

'Oh, Jack, I'm so sorry. Since you knew *you* were not involved, you had to consider that the male who was involved could very well be your father?'

'And from there how was my mother going to feel—react—when all this blew up, as surely it must?'

'I stirred up a whole colony of hornets, didn't I?' Leyne said regretfully.

'In more ways than one,' he replied. He did not expand on that statement, but went on to reveal, 'I had thought—was certain—when I suggested DNA testing, that that would kill the matter dead.'

'But it didn't,' Leyne put in, realising the tremendous shock it must have been to him when the result had come through.

'It didn't,' he agreed. 'And that was mind-blowing enough, before I started to delve into considering all the implications, the uproar, the brouhaha that would ensue should I follow it through.'

'You were unsure what to do for the best?' Leyne suggested—it must have been a thumping great shock to him. For once she half wished she had left everything for Max to sort out.

'Against my more normal practice, I decided to do nothing. To sit on it for a while.'

'But not for very long,' Leyne put in, for all those few weeks of waiting had seen her on an emotional see-saw.

'Not for too long,' he agreed. 'We were having dinner, you and I, when you made it so obvious to me that Pip's father *must* be my father that, taken aback as I was, I could deny the unthinkable no longer.'

'I'm—sorry,' she said again, truly feeling for him.

'Don't be,' Jack said with a disarming smile. 'By the time I was driving you home that night I was starting to take on board that if my father was Pip's father, then that little girl must be my half-sister. Once that was set in my head there was no way—regardless of the fallout—I was going to turn my back on the child.' He gave a half-smile as he added, 'Or her aunt.'

That aunt remark meant nothing. Nor was she going to read anything into it, Leyne decided, even if that half-smile of Jack Dangerfield's did look a shade personal—and made her feel all wobbly inside. 'You—um—wanted to take Pip out to tea the next afternoon,' Leyne commented, more for something to say while she got herself more of one piece than anything.

She did not, however, have the remotest hope of staying in one piece when Jack replied, 'I was taking her nowhere—without her aunt.'

'Oh!' Leyne mumbled. He not only looked a shade personal; he was actually sounding it! And her brain seeming to be functioning on low wattage, 'And—er—that included us going down to Sherbourne with you too, did it?' she asked, more from a sudden need to keep talking than anything.

'Take my word for it,' he answered evenly, his eyes meeting hers, his look steady.

Oh, heavens. 'Max rang,' Leyne erupted out of a complete nowhere. She couldn't handle this. Her imagination was going out of control. She was imagining this was personal, personal to her, when the whole purpose of Jack's visit was in connection with Pip. Only just at the moment she couldn't see how.

Jack favoured her with one of those 'I can see straight through you and your prevarications' type of looks, which Leyne did not very much care for— unless she was imagining that too. Perhaps she was. Because he did not go back to the track he had been on, but enquired, 'Your sister is well now?'

'Yes, thank you. Um—she had some news. Good news.' Leyne felt she was babbling. 'But—'

'I make you nervous, Leyne?' Jack cut in to enquire pleasantly.

'I think I once mentioned—you know too much about women!' Leyne only half succeeded in finding the waspish note she had been after.

'And I think I may have mentioned that you, Leyne Rowberry, are something else again.'

As in, in all his research of the opposite sex, he had never come across one such as her? She very much doubted it. 'Well, there you go,' she threw in, which meant absolutely nothing.

'Would it make you feel any better if I owned that I, too, am feeling a little nervous here?' he enquired quietly.

Leyne stared at him in astonishment. She did not believe that for one single, solitary minute. 'What have *you* got to feel nervous about?' she demanded.

Jack looked levelly at her. 'The same as you, I shouldn't wonder.'

She knew why *she* felt nervous. She was in love with the wretched man, loved him so much she was terrified he might know it or, if he did not know it, that she might somehow slip up and show it. So, since he did not love her, he could not be nervous that *he* might somehow show it. Time, Leyne decided, to back away fast.

'Max is coming home early!' she blurted out.

He smiled. 'That's nice,' he remarked, his eyes, as ever, steady on her.

'She'll be home for Christmas—all being well,' Leyne tacked on hastily.

'Even better.'

'I'm glad you approve.'

His mouth quirked upwards slightly at one corner. 'Why shouldn't I? It will relieve you of having to find a childsitter who won't let you down.'

Ouch! 'That's true,' Leyne replied, somehow wanting to laugh—and wondering if she was getting slightly hysterical.

But Jack's even expression suddenly vanished. 'I

wasn't thinking of the luckless Collins!' he rapped, on seeing her appear to be having pleasing thoughts.

Collins! It staggered Leyne that Jack had remembered Keith's surname. From memory she had only ever mentioned it once. 'Keith's history,' she said off-handedly—and loved it when that seemed to bring a smile to Jack's face.

'I should hope so!' he grunted. And very near sank her when he followed on with, 'Perhaps, when your sister gets home, you'll consider coming out with me?''

Leyne's lips parted in her surprise, and as her heartbeats hurried up she felt a surge of warm colour to her cheeks. He was serious? No? Yes? 'Max is getting married,' she said in a rush. 'In January,' she burbled on. 'Pip and I are going to be bridesmaids.'

'Given that that's no sort of answer to my question, I'm very pleased for her,' he answered, watching, taking note. 'Who's she marrying? Anyone we know?'

Leyne still felt all over the place. Jack wanted to date her! Jack wanted to ask her out! 'Ben Turnbull,' she replied briefly, and would have left it at that. But she caught Jack looking at her, with a—gentle—sort of look in his eyes now, and nervousness was an understatement. Particularly if that look was on account of him having seen how she felt about him. 'Max and Pip will be going to live in

Ben Turnbull's house,' she mentioned, hoping to sidetrack Jack.

'And what about you?' he enquired.

'Max wants me to—well, has asked me to go and live with them. Ben has a large house, apparently.'

'But?' Jack questioned, and Leyne had to smile. How had he known there was a 'but'?

'But I can't see myself doing that. I think they should start their married life, their married family life, without me there.'

'You do?'

'I know I shall miss Max, and I just don't know how I'm going to feel living here without Pip, but—' She broke off. Jack was now looking at her very fixedly, something very intense about his expression. 'What's the matter?' she asked, her voice all kind of staccato as nerves bit again.

'Nothing that I hope can't be put wonderfully right—if I have the answers I want from you,' he replied, to her mind more than somewhat obscurely.

'By the sound of it you have quite a few questions?' Leyne used what brain she could find to frame a halfway intelligent question of her own.

'I was thinking,' Jack said, his tension to her mind in no way easing, 'that I may have a very excellent answer to your problem.'

'I have a problem?'

'Well, you're plainly not looking forward to living on your own,' he replied, and, before she could tell him yea or nay to that, he went on to completely flabbergast her by adding, 'So why not come and live—with me?' And, while she was still doubting her hearing, 'We could have Pip to stay—look after her every time her mother and stepfather want to go off somewhere.' Leyne was still staring at Jack dumbstruck, when, 'What do you say?' he asked.

'You said—live with you?' she checked, staring at him wide-eyed, knowing that her hearing had suddenly gone faulty. It had to have done.

But she was in no way any less astounded, and her hearing none the better, when, with a taut kind of look about him, 'I'll marry you first, naturally,' he told her.

There was a roaring in her ears. He would marry her first? 'W-what did you say?' she managed huskily.

Jack drew a long pulled breath. 'It's coming out too soon,' he muttered. 'I know that. But—' his voice strengthened '—I can't hold back any longer.'

'You—c-can't? she faltered.

He shook his head. 'I can't,' he agreed, and went on to repeat, 'I said that I would marry you first.'

Leyne closed her agape mouth. 'That's what I thought you said,' she uttered faintly. He hadn't asked for that date yet—and here he was *proposing that they marry!* 'Now, why would you want to do that?' she asked, feeling in such strange, unthought territory that she quite desperately needed clarification on just about absolutely everything.

'Because…' Jack began, his eyes on her eyes, refusing to allow her to look away. 'Because…' he said again, and Leyne just could not help wondering then if he really was as nervous as he had intimated. 'Because, ultimately, I'd like you to have my babies.' And, while she stared at him, her eyes enormous, 'And I wouldn't want all the kerfuffle we've been through in connection with Pip when our children near their teenage years.'

Still Leyne stared at him, trying to use what brain power his astonishing statement had left her with. He was suggesting he married her so that any babies they had would know, without having to ask around age eleven, who their father was?

Looking at him, while still not quite believing she had heard what she thought she had heard, 'I—er—don't think that's a very good reason,' she managed faintly, mentally kicking herself for not accepting his offer at face value. There was nothing in the world she would rather do than to go and live with him.

'Well, I could add…' he began, then paused to clear his throat. 'That—I—um—love you.'

Scarlet colour rushed to her face. Had she not been sitting down, she felt she might have fallen down. 'Oh,' she murmured, her voice sounding all kind of croaky. And after a second or two it was still croaky with shock when she added, 'Um—th-that's different.'

'I could also mention that I've been in torment

over you. That when I'm away from you I feel only
half alive. That—' He broke off, a look of strain
there on his face—she wasn't backing away. 'Different?' he queried. 'How so?'

Leyne was in a world she did not quite believe
in. Yet she so wanted to believe in it that the battle
she was having to fight was between the part of her
that loved him, but was still afraid of him seeing her
love, and the fact that—incredibly—if she could
believe him, Jack was saying that he loved her.

She drew a very shaky breath, and grabbed at a
moment of courage to explain, her voice as shaky as
she felt, 'Well, I wouldn't marry you—without love,'
and waited, her small moment of courage spent, to
see him either burst out laughing that she had taken
him seriously or for whatever else he might say.

What he did was to smile an encouraging half-
smile—a smile that seemed to say that he, on his
part, had been encouraged by her answer. 'You do
love me, then?' he enquired.

'Did I say I would marry you?'

'Yes,' he lied—without hesitation he lied. 'Yes,
you did.' He compounded that first lie.

Not only did she feel on shaky ground now, the
ground was positively crumbling beneath her feet.
'W-well, I—um—wouldn't want to make a liar of
you,' she commented huskily, her colour still high.

Barely had the words left her than Jack was on
his feet. 'Come here and say that,' he instructed.

She stayed where she was. 'To be honest, Jack, you've sort of—er—knocked me sideways, and I'm not certain my legs will hold me.'

'I'll hold you, willingly,' he answered, and came over to her, bending, reaching down for her. Gently he drew her from her chair. 'I've wanted to hold you, oh, so much,' he breathed, taking her unresisting form in his arms and holding her to him 'It seems light years away since I was close to you.' He pulled back to look into her face. 'You love me?' he asked.

And for Leyne then it was a case of all or nothing. Either she made all effort to pretend he was mistaken or, since from what she knew of him she felt he would not be holding her in his arms unless she was safe, and—could trust him. 'You—guessed?' she plunged.

'I hoped,' he answered. 'I thought, when you were ready to give yourself to me, that you might love me a little. But, against that, I have never, ever felt about anyone the way I feel about you, so there were many more times when I was certain I was mistaken, and that I must be off my head to imagine you might care for me.'

'Oh,' she murmured softly, 'you *do* feel something for me.'

Jack looked down into her shining eyes. 'Sweet Leyne, how could I not? You're brave and adorable. Is it any wonder that I love you quite to distraction?'

'Oh,' she whispered. And he bent and gently kissed her. She reached for him, steadied herself with her hands at his waist, her confidence in him, in his love, starting to grow. 'And—er—wh-when did this phenomenon begin?' she enquired solemnly.

'When did you begin to be my moon, my stars, my world?' He gently kissed her again—her arms went round him—he had not the smallest objection. 'Looking back, I believe something started to happen in me that day you planted yourself straight in front of me and promptly informed me that I was the father of an eleven-year-old.'

'I think I was desperate.'

'You were sensational,' he responded. 'The best aunt any niece could want. And, given that I was not her father, we both know now that you were in the right family area—' He broke off and, as if compelled, asked, 'Love me, Leyne?'

Love words did not come easily to her. In fact she had never uttered them in this context before. 'Er—some,' she answered, but was relieved when Jack seemed to understand, for the pressure of his arms tightened a little and he smiled an encouraging smile.

But, as if endeavouring to make her feel more and more comfortable with him, he continued, 'So there was I, fully realising that I should dismiss this mad if beautiful woman who'd accosted me from my mind—only to find that I could not.'

'You couldn't?' Leyne loved the way he was

tenderly looking at her. Loved to be in his arms. He was serious. He loved her! *Her!*

'I just could not,' he confirmed.

Leyne's confidence took another leap. 'You instead found the letter I'd written?' she suggested.

'Yvonne did. And also noted my instruction to put you through should you ring.'

'You knew I would?'

He kissed her again, purely because he could not resist his need to do so. 'I thought you might,' he agreed when he drew back. 'I knew without question that you couldn't pin the "father" label on me, and that I could prove it any time I cared. But, in spite of myself, I was intrigued.'

'About Pip's parentage?'

Jack shook his head. 'Not then. I hadn't then met the green-eyed, raven-haired little sweetheart with everything about her screaming out that she is a Dangerfield. Back then, I confess it was more because I couldn't get this Leyne Rowberry out of my head than anything that I found I was giving you a call and then coming to see you.'

Leyne felt that if her heart beat any faster it would burst. She had intrigued him? Way back then! It was all more than a little mind-blowing. She fought for, and found, a tiny thread of something sensible. 'You suggested DNA,' she recalled. 'Even though you knew in advance that you were not Pip's father.'

'There was something about you, my darling,' he

said, and that 'my darling' turned her bones to water. 'It refused to let me sever all connection with you that day. Which it would have been if I had told you the truth.'

'That you were in Australia when Pip was conceived?' Leyne filled in.

Jack smiled. 'I was just about to tell you exactly that when I made the mistake of looking at you—and the words just would not come.'

'Oh,' she sighed, and didn't know where she was for a moment or two. But, recalling that morning, 'You must have been shaken rigid when the DNA results came through showing a blood link?'

'And then some,' he endorsed. 'Though it wasn't long before I started to be very taken with my little sister and…' He paused, and smiled a smile of such love that Leyne had to grip hard on to him. He seemed to like it, because he was smiling still as he owned, '…and quickly realised that I wanted to see more and more of her aunt.' His look became rueful as he revealed, 'It wasn't long before I began to realise that I was in deep trouble.'

'Over—me?'

'You, sweet love,' he agreed. 'That first Friday when I came to collect you, to take you and Pip down to Sherbourne, I stood in the doorway of your study watching your lovely serious face—and you looked over. I said for you to take as much time as you needed, but it was I who needed time, to get myself back together again from the adrenaline rush I'd experienced just to see you again.'

Leyne stared at him incredulously. 'Honestly?' she gasped.

'That was just the start,' Jack assured her. 'The next morning we were walking on the beach and I looked at you—and suddenly my chest is thumping, you're the most beautiful woman in the world, and I'm having to fight like the devil not to take you in my arms and kiss you.'

'Oh, Jack,' Leyne whispered, and realised that her confidence must have escalated higher and higher, because she just had to reach up and kiss him.

It was as if that was what he had been waiting for. Because all at once he was gathering her closer and yet closer to him, and he was kissing her with an ardour that left her breathless.

Her colour was high when he pulled back. 'I'm sorry, my darling, it's just that I feel starved for your kisses.'

She smiled up at him; she just could not help it. 'Please don't apologise,' she said, adding impishly, 'I quite enjoyed it.'

He grinned back. 'Love me?'

'You know I do.'

'Am I ever going to hear you say it?'

'I…' was as far as she got, before shyness to say those special words came and tripped her up. 'That was a good weekend—given that Pip had a small asthma attack.'

'It was to discuss Pip's asthma in private that I came to your room early the next morning.'

'You kissed me then,' Leyne recalled dreamily.

He had not forgotten—nor any word that had passed between them that Sunday morning, it seemed—for he instantly recalled, 'You told me not to go overboard. Your warning, my love, came a little too late.'

'How?' she asked, totally fascinated.

'I fear I was already lost. And knew it for a fact an hour or so later, when you told me you didn't want an affair with me.'

'You didn't spare my blushes on that one.' Leyne remembered every word *he* had said on that issue, without having to think about it. 'You made it abundantly plain that an affair with me was the last thing on your mind.'

'And so it was,' Jack declared. And went on to stagger her some more by openly stating, 'I didn't want an *affair* with you, dear, dear Leyne. I knew that very morning that what I did want was to marry you.'

Leyne stared at him spellbound. 'You knew *then*! You knew then that...' Words failed her.

'My very dear love, I knew then that you were the woman I wanted to spend the rest of my life with. I knew then that I was deeply in love with you.

That I loved you with my whole being—and that where you were was where I wanted to be.'

'Oh—Jack,' Leyne murmured shakenly. 'But—but I never so much as guessed!'

'How could you? And how could I have done anything about it then? I hadn't tackled my father on the subject of Pip. There was my mother to consider. And that was before we got around to your family and how your sister was going to feel about any of it. And all that before I could begin to get to the very big issue of how did you feel about me, and what were my chances if I tried to come a-courting?'

'I had no idea you were feeling, thinking, that way!' Leyne gasped.

'You don't know the half of it,' Jack replied feelingly. 'To say I've been in torment is an understatement!'

'Over me?' She could scarcely believe it.

'You've had me sleepless too many nights,' he informed her. 'Last night, in particular, I felt I was in danger of going off my head. I'd phoned you twice, about to ask you out on a date—you didn't want to know.'

He had phoned on Wednesday, and again last night, she instantly recalled, staring at him wordlessly. 'But—but you never said!'

'You were too busy batting off other offers. I decided—in my bruised pride—that I was certain I had no interest in joining the long line of your suitors.'

'Bruised pride?' she queried—and suddenly something clicked. 'You were jealous!' she exclaimed in wonder.

He gave a self-deprecating grin. 'I've known every shade of green,' he admitted.

'Oh, Jack,' she sighed. And had to admit, 'I've been jealous too.'

He liked that, and looked deeply into her eyes. 'Sweet love,' he murmured, and gently kissed her. 'You do love me, then?'

Leyne looked lovingly back at him. 'I'm so glad you're here,' she said simply. 'It has been painful without you.'

Jack kissed her again, as if to kiss away any pain she had known, any pain which he might have unknowingly inflicted. 'I'm glad I'm here too,' he breathed. 'Glad that, when I knew I could not endure another night of wakeful torture, I decided to come and try and get through the barriers you had put up.'

'Barriers?'

'You're trying to pretend you haven't been trying to freeze me out?'

'Freeze you out?' Leyne asked, startled.

'You were colder than charity last Sunday. I thought—'

'You—you were aloof!' Leyne exclaimed.

'Me?' He seemed surprised, but on reflection accepted, 'Perhaps I was.' He gave a small shrug. 'A man has his pride, and you were showing, quite plainly, that you were regretting you had been on the brink of giving yourself to me the day before.'

Colour flew to her cheeks, though she could not deny the truth of what he was saying. 'I—um—have my pride too,' she said quietly. 'I thought I might have given away—a—um—hint of what I feel for you.'

A slow smile started to spread across his features. 'And, given that I love you with everything that's in me, how would that be, my darling?' he asked.

'Like—I have had my sleepless nights too.'

His smile became a delighted grin. 'We're getting there,' he encouraged.

'Like—you fill my head, even when you *are* being aloof with me.'

'Oh, I've been there, little Leyne Rowberry,' he said ruefully. 'In my case, it's called love.'

She smiled at him. 'Mine too,' she admitted. 'It—just happened. Was there! And there wasn't one single solitary thing I could do about it.'

'So, what do you suppose you could call that?' he asked.

Her smile became a grin, a dreamy grin. 'Love,' she agreed. And suddenly she just had to tell him, 'Oh, Jack Dangerfield, I love you. So very much.'

'My darling!' he exclaimed, and, holding her close, teased tenderly, 'Now, that didn't hurt so very much, did it?'

She shook her head, feeling choked suddenly. 'Not any more,' she whispered.

Gently, he kissed her. 'Marry me? You *will* marry me?' he urged.

'Whenever you say,' she replied.

'How do you fancy being your sister's matron of honour?'

'Max wants me to be her bridesmaid.'

'Bridesmaids aren't married. Matrons of honour are.'

'But—but—Max is getting married in January!'

'You think I can wait that long to make you Mrs Jack Dangerfield?'

'Oh, Jack,' Leyne whispered.

'Oh, Jack, yes?'

'Yes, yes, yes!' she laughed breathlessly.

They looked wondrously into each other's eyes—and just had to kiss.

MILLS & BOON®

Live the emotion

Romance

HER CHRISTMAS WEDDING WISH
by Judy Christenberry

Workaholic attorney Richard Anderson's life changed when he became guardian to his orphaned nephew. He tried hard, but it was up to Molly, the boy's beautiful nurse, to make this a very special Christmas...

MARRIED UNDER THE MISTLETOE
by Linda Goodnight

When Daniel Stephens finds out who his real father is, he learns that he's part of the Valentine dynasty. He's not convinced that he fits into their world...until he meets Bella Lucia manager Stephanie Ellison... Could this be a Christmas to remember for both of them?

SNOWBOUND REUNION *by Barbara McMahon*

Cath Morgan has decided to spend Christmas alone, away from the city and her husband Jake. For six years Cath has dreamed of more from her marriage. But Jake isn't about to give up. He has one Christmas to show how much he loves Cath and to make their marriage beautiful again...

THE TYCOON'S INSTANT FAMILY *by Caroline Anderson*

When business tycoon Nick Barron hires Georgie Cauldwell, they spend a few romantic weeks together. Then Nick disappears, returning with two young children and a tiny baby. Georgie shouldn't fall in love with a man with a family – but there is something about this family she can't resist...

On sale 3rd November 2006

BCC/AD 2006 a

**breast
cancer
CAMPAIGN**

researching the cure

The facts you need to know:

- Breast cancer is the commonest form of cancer in the United Kingdom. **One woman in nine** will develop the disease during her lifetime.

- Each year around **41,000** women and approximately **300** men are diagnosed with breast cancer and around **13,000** women and **90** men will die from the disease.

- 80% of all breast cancers occur in post-menopausal women and approximately 8,200 pre-menopausal women are diagnosed with the disease each year.

- However, survival rates are improving, with on average 77.5% of women diagnosed between 1996 and 1999 still alive five years later, compared to 72.8% for women diagnosed between 1991 and 1996.

Breast Cancer Campaign is the only charity that specialises in funding independent breast cancer research throughout the UK. It aims to find the cure for breast cancer by funding research which looks at improving diagnosis and treatment of breast cancer, better understanding how it develops and ultimately either curing the disease or preventing it.

All you could want for Christmas!

Meet handsome and seductive men under the mistletoe, escape to the world of Regency romance or simply relax by the fire with a heartwarming tale by one of our bestselling authors. These special stories will fill your holiday with Christmas sparkle!

Christmas Treasures

BETTY NEELS

CAROLINE ANDERSON
HELEN BROOKS

On sale 6th October 2006

CHRISTMAS Proposals

CAROLE MORTIMER
REBECCA WINTERS
MARION LENNOX

THREE NEW CHRISTMAS ROMANCES

You're all he wants for Christmas

A CHRISTMAS Hero

RACHEL LEE, MARLENE LOVELACE
CATHERINE MANN

MILLS & BOON

Regency

LORDS & LADIES CHRISTMAS

Nicola Cornick &
Lyn Stone, Julia Justiss

On sale 20th October 2006

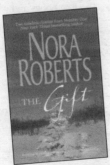

4 FREE

BOOKS AND A SURPRISE GIFT!

We would like to take this opportunity to thank you for reading this Mills & Boon® book by offering you the chance to take FOUR more specially selected titles from the Romance series absolutely FREE! We're also making this offer to introduce you to the benefits of the Mills & Boon® Reader Service™—

- ★ **FREE home delivery**
- ★ **FREE gifts and competitions**
- ★ **FREE monthly Newsletter**
- ★ **Exclusive Reader Service offers**
- ★ **Books available before they're in the shops**

Accepting these FREE books and gift places you under no obligation to buy, you may cancel at any time, even after receiving your free shipment. Simply complete your details below and return the entire page to the address below. You don't even need a stamp!

YES! Please send me 4 free Romance books and a surprise gift. I understand that unless you hear from me, I will receive 6 superb new titles every month for just £2.80 each, postage and packing free. I am under no obligation to purchase any books and may cancel my subscription at any time. The free books and gift will be mine to keep in any case.

N6ZED

Ms/Mrs/Miss/Mr ....Initials ....

BLOCK CAPITALS PLEASE

Surname ....

Address ....

....

....Postcode.............................

Send this whole page to:
UK: FREEPOST CN81, Croydon, CR9 3WZ